MW01519068

The Running Man

A novel

W. A. Harbinson

Author's Note

The Running Man is an early work of mine, originally published in 1967 as a Horwitz Books original paperback, as part of a package of four short novels that I wrote on commission while living in a rented apartment in Katoomba, a town located 68 miles west of Sydney, overlooking the spectacular Blue Mountain range. Of the four novels I wrote there in a very short time (about six weeks), *The Running Man* was the only one that could be considered to be about a serious subject. The commissioning editor, Ron Smith, didn't really want a serious subject from me (he specialised in largely male-interest comedies) and I'm convinced that he really only accepted it as a special favour to me because I was about to leave Australia for good and head off for London. How surprising, therefore, that this was one of the few Horwitz novels to later be published in both Britain and America. It was then adapted as a small-budget 'art house' movie entitled *The City's Edge*, directed by Ken Quinnel, starring Hugo Weaver, Tommy Lewis and Katrina Foster. It was the only one of my many subsequent novels, including my bestsellers, to receive such treatment.

Despite being written for what might rightfully be described as a potboiler publisher, I have always believed that this short novel has real literary merit. When writing an Afterword to a later, more literary novel of mine, *Knock*, Colin Wilson, in a brief overview of my career, said of *The Running Man*: 'The plot is melodramatic and at times incredible, but the novel has real power and conviction.' Despite my personal reservations and, perhaps, adding substance to Wilson's claim, when the film adaptation of the novel was released in the United States in 1983, it was described by *Variety* as 'the first Australian feature which explores the dilemma of the urban Aboriginal.' So something worthwhile might have come out of it.

Here, then, after all these years, is a slightly revised new edition of *The Running Man*, one of my very first novels. Enjoy reading it. I certainly enjoyed writing it.

W. A. Harbinson
West Cork, Ireland
2016

The Running Man

Chapter One

THE RUNNING MAN

When my father died, choking up blood and words of contempt for me, I quickly packed and got the hell out of there. I didn't even wait for the funeral. My mother was weeping, my sister was in hysterics, my kid brother was getting plastered in the local boozer and I just walked out. No goodbyes. Nothing. Out and away.

I got a second-class seat on the train out of Perth and I talked to no one. Beyond plate-glass windows the awful barren wastes of the Nullarbor Plain swept past like a vision in a dying man's final dream. I got methodically drunk on a bottle of Johnny Walker. I didn't want to think about my father, so I bought another bottle at Adelaide and kept at it. Some of the other passengers were looking at me, but I didn't give a damn. When the train pulled into Melbourne, it was raining and I couldn't help but imagine the funeral with that stark black hole in the earth and all the despised relatives in mock mourning. Talking about me, no doubt.

I knew damned well what they'd be saying about me: that I was a coward, a drifter, a dreamer of much talk and little action, that I would get nowhere fast – that I was a disgrace to the family. Well, this time I would show them.

Dipping into my diminishing bank account, I stayed on in Melbourne for a few days. What for, I'll never know. It rained the whole time. The sky was black, the streets were grey, and depression dragged me back to the bottle.

In a bleak room in St. Kilda I made love to a whore who looked through me as if I was made of glass. The next day, I took her to Shepard's bar where I stared at the paintings on the walls and vomited on the floor. When they threw me out, I bid the whore goodbye and booked into the YMCA. Then I lay flat on my back for three days and tried not to think of my dead dad. Rich old man who loved most of his family but could never understand me because I wanted to be a Great Writer and didn't write anything. I had tried to tell him: 'Dad, it's all building. I just have to work it out.' But I was twenty-five years old, I'd been expelled from university, I'd lived off his handouts ever since, so he no longer wanted to know me.

'You're a wastrel,' he'd said.

On the third morning I finally got out of bed and went down to the cafeteria for breakfast. After trying a boiled egg I had to rush to the toilet where I made a terrible mess in a clean sink. By ten the same morning I was again on the booze and by three that afternoon I was in the custody of the cops. They let me go with a warning, so I collected my gear from the YMCA and hopped the evening train to Sydney. I felt as if I'd been on the move all my life.

'I'm not a wastrel,' I said to myself. 'I am *not* a wastrel!'

When I saw some other passengers staring at me, I shut my fat mouth.

I had always wanted to see Sydney, but when I finally arrived it terrified me. I wandered through those

10

teeming streets with my single bag in one hand and my portable typewriter in the other. I looked at the traffic and the endless streams of people and I felt so alone I was almost sick again. Once I smiled at a girl. She turned glacial eyes toward me, then turned away as if to wither me – and it did. I actually blushed and hurried away, furtively, feeling like some kind of pervert.

I hailed a taxi.

'Where to, fella?'

'I want a room. Somewhere in King's Cross.'

'Who doesn't?'

The room I found was in a dilapidated rooming house in the busy, neon-lit King's Cross Road. I was feeling pretty seamy and this room made me feel right at home. There was a bed, a chest of drawers, two wooden chairs and a cold-water sink. A single small gas ring enabled me to boil coffee. The old bag who showed me in had a darkly suspicious look in her eyes (by this time I must have looked a right mess), so I paid her for a fortnight in advance. Then I unpacked and went out to look at the fabled Cross.

I had been reading about the Cross for years, so I expected something fabulous or exciting to happen during my first evening there. I walked up and down, looking at the neon signs, the strip clubs, the coffee bars, the pubs and shops and women, but nothing happened. Except that it started to rain, just as it had done in Melbourne. So I went back to my room, lay on the bed, stared up at the ceiling and tried desperately not to think about my dad.

Then I cried for the first time.

Chapter Two

ROOMING HOUSE

After my first miserable evening in the Cross, I determined to lock myself up in my room, speak to no one, and grimly work on the long-promised novel that would smack my miserable relatives right between the eyes. Had it not been for the fact that during my first attempt to sleep in my new bed I suffered a nightmare, I might have succeeded.

I was a child again, held firmly in warm arms, while being lowered, face down, into the deep black hole of my father's grave. It was damp and cold down there. I could smell the rot. A voice on the wind told me to kiss the lips that were not, in actual fact, to be cold for another twenty years. Looking down, I saw my father's eyes as two huge glassy orbs, and when I looked at his lips, I saw that they were alive with a slimy, slithering mass of fat worms. 'Kiss him,' said that voice blown in on the wind, and then invisible hands were pushing my child's face down on his. I tried to protest but couldn't, my tongue was numb, and all I had left was the strength to struggle. This I did, but I was revolted, terrified, and so I wriggled and kicked frantically, but in vain. I kept going down, down, onto that hideous mass of slithering warms – and then I finally found my voice, I screamed, screamed myself back to consciousness, to the sight of a stream of fire pouring into the room and a man trying to shake me awake.

'Hey, mate, hey!' he said, gently lowering me back to the pillow as my screaming subsided to a sweaty silence. 'Take it easy…'

'Get out,' I said.

'What?'

'I said, get out.'

'Take it easy, fella, you've had a bad time.'

'I don't need your help.'

'That's what we all say.'

I hadn't locked my room door. Now it was fully open and what I had thought was a stream of fire was just the light pouring in from the landing outside. The face of the man standing above me was erased by this light; the rest of him was hidden by the darkness. But he was a slim, small squirt and I didn't like him just for being there. I had fallen asleep fully clothed and sweat was sticking to me.

'I'm sorry,' I said.

'What for?'

'For ordering you out.'

'Think nothing of it. Here, have a drink. It'll help to steady you down.'

I saw a bottle of Haig Dimple dangling from the pale hand before me. I was just about to make a grab for it, automatically, but then I checked myself.

'I don't drink much,' I said.

'You don't smell like it.'

'Well, I'm not an alcoholic. Just get that into your head. I'm *not* an alcoholic!'

'Take it easy, fella,' he repeated. 'Quit shouting. So, you got drunk. Who doesn't now and then? All I'm offering is a hair of the dog that bit you. Here, have a sip. It'll pick you up. Steady your nerves.'

'My father recently died,' I said, and instantly despised myself for saying it.

'I'm sorry.'

'You sound like you actually mean that.'

'What if I don't? What else would you *expect* me to say?'

'Nothing. Thanks.'

'Drink? Yes or no?'

'Yes.'

I took the bottle from him and had a good stiff shot. My belly burned, my eyes watered, but after quickly having a second shot I felt a lot better. 'Thanks,' I said, handing the bottle back to him.

'Cigarette?' he asked.

'What are you? The Salvation Army?'

'Not quite. I live here and you can't escape, so I can always get back what I give. Mind if I sit on the edge of your bed? You're safe because I'm straight.'

'Help yourself.'

He sat down and passed over a cigarette. We lit up and then puffed in silence for a few minutes. He was deliberately casual when he asked, 'What were you screaming about?'

'The Bogey man.'

'An old friend of mine. What else were you screaming about?'

'You're pretty persistent.'

'Why not? If you don't want to answer, all you've got to do is say *no*.'

'I was dreaming about my dad. In his grave. You happy now?'

'Indifferent.'

'Then why ask me in the first place?'

'Just to make conversation and keep you awake. At least until you've had a few more drinks. Otherwise, you're liable to start screaming again and waken half the house. You might as well know, you're almost famous already. That scream of yours is unique.'

'They all heard me?'

'I think, yes. *All* of them.'

'I haven't heard any complaints.'

'You won't. They get all sorts here.'

'Who are they?'

'The sad, the lost, the lonely, the crazy, the nice and the not-so-nice. A most original bunch, myself included.'

'You sound pretty jaded.'

'In the daylight, I look it.'

'What do you do?'

'I'm an alcoholic. And I don't mind admitting it.'

'I repeat: I'm *not.*'

'Didn't say you were. Why do you keep mentioning it?'

'Alright, forget it.'

'Forgotten. Listen: here they all scream, if not in their sleep, in their minds. They might mention your screaming, but only like they'd mention the weather.'

'Who's worried?'

'You are.'

'I'll avoid them,'

'You can't. This rooming house is too small.'

'Do you do anything else, other than drinking?'

'Yes.'

'What?'

'Beg for the money to drink *with.*'

'Are you about to bite me?'

'Not yet. I have enough to keep me going for a few more days. If you're gone by then, you'll escape unscathed.'

'I can't believe you're an alcoholic.'

'No one ever does until they get to know me. Now, it only shows in my eyes.'

'What are they like?'

'You'll see in the morning.'

'You're leaving now?'

'Yes.'

'What's your name?'

'Wentworth. James Oliver Wentworth. You may call me Jim.'

'Andy White here.'

'Welcome, Andy White. But sooner or later, you'll regret having come here.'

'What's your age, Jim?'

'What do you think?'

'I'm bad on ages. Somewhere between thirty and forty.'

'Twenty-three. Goodnight.'

He left, closing the door quietly behind him.

*   *   *

I didn't sleep through the rest of that long, hallowed morning. I was frightened and I didn't know why. I kept thinking of my father's grave and of James Oliver Wentworth's elliptical conversation. Of course, it was a joke that he was only twenty-three years old – a sour joke, maybe, but a joke for all that. I had seen his face when he sat down on the edge of the bed: youthful but rough, all deep lines and despair, with hints of grey in his receding hairline. The face of a long and bitter experience: straight from the womb into a liquor bottle, smiling, not at, but in, defeat. No normal man could look like that a twenty-three. Not even me. And I'd had enough troubles to wreck anyone. Yet how long had it been since I'd really looked into the mirror?

'Have a good look at yourself some day,' my father had said before he died. 'At twenty-five you're already dissolute.'

'That's a lie,' I now answered aloud to the room. Then I reached over to the chest of drawers and snatched another cigarette from the packet. I wanted to hide.

*   *   *

I neither found a place to hide nor a moment in which to sleep. The following morning, shortly after a red dawn, James Oliver Wentworth came back into my room and said, 'I knew you wouldn't be asleep, kid. My room's right next to yours, so I could hear you pacing all night. Here, have another nip. Temporarily, I feel my proper and sprightly age of twenty-three.'

'I thought that was a joke.'

'Not every merciful, are you?'

'I don't like your attitude.'

'Which is?'

'I don't know, but I don't like it.'

'I'll accept that. Now have an early-morning snort.'

I took the bottle from him, tilted it at him in a mock salute, grinned mockingly and said, 'Here's to your twenty-three years.'

'Sticks and stones, pal.'

As he flipped a cigarette into his mouth, he glanced around the room with clear distaste. Then, lighting the cigarette, he glanced down at me and shook his head from side to side.

'You don't look like you belong in this dive,' he said.

After knocking back some of the Haig Dimple, I wiped my wet lips with the back of my free hand and said, 'I'll get used to it.'

'God help you when you do. It'll mean you finally belong – and that's the bitter end. I set myself up as a shining example.'

'Twenty-three?'

'Not a year older.'

'Then you're an example.'

He took the bottle from me and had a drink. 'Ah, lovely!' he said, then looking directly at me, he added, 'You can't be superior when under the same roof. You got a record?'

'What?'

'A criminal record.'

'No.'

'Woman trouble?'

'None that I'd run from.'

'Then what are you doing here? With the alcoholic peepers?'

'I might ask the same of you.'

'I'd have no answer.'

'That's *my* answer.'

He slapped one of his knees, again glanced around the room, rubbed his unshaven chin with the palm of his right hand. In his oddly wasted way he was still close to handsome and I saw that, indeed, beneath the tarnished appearance he had the face of someone only slightly younger than myself. It gave me the shivers. So young to be so damned old. He was wearing light-blue denims, an old duffle coat, a checkered shirt. His cigarette dangled loosely from slack lips.

'What are you plans, kid?' he asked.

'I'm a couple of years older than you, so you can drop the *kid* bit.'

'Then what do I call you?'

'I told you last night.'

'My memory's not the best.'

'Andy.'

'So what are your plans, Andy?'

I could have said any one of a dozen things, but I didn't. I looked around my sparse, gloomy room and thought of the long, lonely day ahead. Staring at my typewriter as if it was about to eat me, I said, 'None in particular.'

'Feel like seeing the place?'

'You don't have to put yourself out.'

'I don't do favours, believe me. I've just got to get out of this place or I'll go mad.'

'I don't want to spend all day drinking.'

'You can drop out of the tour whenever you wish. Are you coming or aren't you?'

'I'm coming.'

'Okay. Have a wash and a shave and then come into my room, right next door. I'll have a pot of coffee on the boil. Any breakfast is better than no breakfast at all. See you in a few minutes.'

When he left the room, taking the bottle with him, I slid off the bed. I stayed there for a moment, swaying, silently suffering my thick head and heaving stomach. I'd been drinking for so long now, I'd forgotten what it was like to be sober. Dragging my travel bag from under the bed, I heaved it on top of the blankets and began to go through it for a clean shirt and my shaving kit. As I did this, I recalled saying to Wentworth that I didn't drink much. I wondered why I had said that.

*   *   *

'You ready?' Wentworth shouted from the adjoining room.

'I'm just unpacking!'

'Well, get a move on!'

Draping a towel around my neck and taking the shaving kit in my right hand, I left the room to find the bathroom. The landing was gloomy, my nostrils inhaled the dust, there was an aroma of old urine and general decay in the air. I went down a flight of creaking stairs, along a short corridor, and turned left into the bathroom. No sooner had I closed the door behind me than a loud, solid hammering resounded from it, and a peculiar, high-pitched voice shrieked, 'Come on! Come on! I don't have all morning! Get a move on!'

'I've just walked in!' I shouted back out, not feeling amused.

'Don't you have a job to go to?'

'What's it to you?'

'Ah, I thought not. No one in this hell-hole has honest employment, except this poor old cripple, who shouldn't have to work in the first place. No employment, no responsibilities, no deadlines to keep. All a lot of bodgies – and you insist upon making *me* late for work.' He hammered again on the door, this time with what sounded like a walking stick, and then added, '*Move!*'

'Shut your mouth!' I responded, and then another voice, sounding very much like that of the old bag who ran this dump, joined the bedlam by repeating what the first voice had said. 'You've been in there long enough!' she bawled. 'Give someone else a go!'

The protests died down shortly after, but as I shaved myself I could hear the man at the other side of the door shuffling impatiently and muttering under his breath. Every so often he would tap lightly on the door with his stick and enquire, with forced politeness, 'Are you *nearly* finished?' I chose not to reply. In the magnifying mirror in front of me, I couldn't see any more than the smallest portion of my reflected face at any time, mostly only my chin. This actually relieved me. When you're born handsome, you soon start feeling like the dessert on every cannibal's plate; after a while, your own face becomes a taunt to you. Relief it was, then, when I finished shaving, dried my face, and opened the bathroom door.

'Morning,' I said.

Staring at me was the ugliest face I had ever seen. The man was indeed a cripple: a hunchback. He was wearing dirty striped pyjamas. The expression on his repulsive face was one of open contempt.

'The name's Fields,' he said. 'Don't ever forget it. I despise you as much as you loathe me.'

Then he rushed past me, into the bathroom, slamming the door closed behind him.

'Looks like you made a friend, darlin',' said a clearly amused female voice. Turning around, I saw a middle-aged woman leaning against the door frame of her room, attired in a faded dressing gown, languidly filing her fingernails and smiling, as if to herself. Shoulder-length fell artfully over one of her mocking eyes. Apart from this piece of calculated erotic subterfuge, there was nothing especially attractive about her.

'Looks like it,' I said.

'You just moved in, handsome?'

'Yes.'

'Alone?'

'Yes.'

'You ever need company?'

'Sometimes.'

'You're not one of the *other* kind, are you?'

I grinned. 'Not to the best of my knowledge.'

'Pleased to hear it. Anytime you're in need, handsome, just knock on my door. I'm always available.'

'Is that an invitation?'

'It's a proposition. There's a difference.'

'I'll keep it in mind.'

'Bless you, darlin'.'

Stepping past her, I climbed the stairs and returned to my room. Wentworth was already sitting on the edge of my bed, his legs nonchalantly crossed, a glazed look in his bloodshot eyes. He had placed two cups of steaming black coffee on the chest of drawers. Between sips of his own cup, he was drinking from another bottle of Haig Dimple. A very good Scotch whisky.

'Don't you ever stop drinking?' I asked him.

'It happens. On occasion.'

'How did it start?'

'Would you like a tragic story or an honest one?'

'I'll settle for the truth.'

'I acquired a taste for it. That's all.'

When I finished buttoning my shirt, I had a sip of the coffee. It almost scalded my throat, but cleared my head a little. For such small mercies I felt pitifully grateful.

I, too, had been drinking too much, too long. I started when I was told that my dad, who despised me, was dying. When he finally died, I was still at it – and still at it when I caught the train out of Adelaide. I'd never known before that I loved him. Suddenly and too late.

'You ready?' I asked Wentworth.

'Sorry, we can't go. Not until tonight. I just remembered something.'

'What?'

'This is visiting day.'

'Who do you visit and where?'

'I'm afraid I'm the inmate and the one who comes to see me is my sister. Little Miss Protector. Without whom I would die.'

'When does she arrive?'

'Some time today.'

'What do we do in the meantime?'

'We drink with esteemed company. Come! I'll introduce you. But I warn you here and now: you're about to join the company of the damned.'

* * *

'I've already met your friend, thank you,' the hunchback said, 'and under the most unsociable circumstances. He held me up, he kept me waiting – deliberately, I believe– and I'm afraid I don't like him one bit. Kindly leave my room. I am dressing and must soon be off to work. Do you know what work is?'

'Mr. Fields,' Wentworth began, 'it was simply an accident – '

'Everything's an accident,' Fields interjected. 'The whole miserable world is an accident. *I'm* an accident. Who forgives me?'

'Mr. Fields, I just forgot to tell him about you and the order we have in using the bathroom. You first, of course.'

'Me being the only one in this building with a proper job. But who remembers me?'

'He's new here, Mr. Fields. You can't be unfriendly.'

'Name?'

'White,' I said. 'Andy White.'

'Horace Fields,' he responded, abruptly offering his hand. We shook. Then he went back to checking himself in the mirror on the wall. I couldn't keep my eyes off his legs, which twisted like those of a crippled spider. 'Truck,' he said, noticing the direction of my gaze. 'When I was a child. You needn't pretend I'm normal.'

'I'll try not to.'

23

'Good. You ignore my deformities and I'll ignore yours.'

'I don't have any.'

'Examine that statement.'

Having completed the knotting of his tie, he put on the jacket of his businessman's suit and hobbled to the side of the bed. On the bed was an open suitcase filled with children's toys. 'I make them myself,' he said. 'Down in the basement. Then I stand all day in Darlinghurst Road, selling them mostly to drunken grown-ups, the parents of the ghastly little brats who attend nearby schools. I never give change unless it's asked for. Dishonest, maybe, but at least I do *work* for a living. Now I must be off.'

Taking his now closed suitcase in one hand, his walking stick in the other, he ushered me and Wentworth out of the room. Following us out, he carefully shut and locked the door, then, muttering under his breath, he hobbled away to another day's bitter business.

'He sounds crazy,' I said to Wentworth.

'He *is* crazy. He works precisely from nine to five every day, selling those awful toys. Then, at five every evening, he goes into the nearest pub and proceeds to get plastered. After a couple of beers, accompanied by whisky chasers, he starts swinging his walking stick at anyone coming within range. He foams at the mouth, he babbles incoherently, but someone, a drinking mate, always kindly brings him back here and puts him to bed. He thinks we're all worthless because we don't work and he demands first place in the bathroom queue because he *does* work. He seems to hate everything and everyone – including himself. Otherwise, he's harmless.'

We stopped at another open door. Inside, the room was cluttered with paintings and an artist's working tools. A tall, thin young man with a red beard and watery eyes was standing thoughtfully in front of an unfinished painting on an easel. The painting vaguely resembled Dante's Inferno as portrayed by William Blake. It wasn't easy to look at.

'Henry Williams, meet our latest resident, Andy White.'

Williams turned around, put out a limp hand, fluttered his eyelashes and said, 'Why, good day, sweetie!'

When we shook hands, I noticed that Williams hung on for longer than was strictly necessary. I stepped back with some haste.

A slight, mocking smile flickered on Williams' face. 'Do you plan to stay here long?' he asked.

'Don't know,' I replied.

'I hope you do, pet.'

'Thanks.'

'Believe me, sweetie, it was a purely selfish remark. Watch out for that bitch downstairs; I don't believe she's clean.'

'I have no plans for her.'

'Oh, good.' And Williams smiled again.

When we left the room, Wentworth informed me that Williams wasn't a homosexual. He just acted that way. Wentworth then knocked on another closed door and announced himself by shouting through it. A deep voice responded with, 'Come in,' and we entered the room of Jack Collins.

*   *   *

Collins was lethargically stretched out between two deep armchairs, legs raised, head back, a transistor radio pressed to his right ear. He had short legs, a broad, well-muscled body, and a battered, cynical, intelligent face. A cigarette dangled from between thick lips. He squinted at us from behind drifting veils of smoke, and then his dark, leathery skin crinkled around a lazy grin.

'Who's your friend?' he asked.

Wentworth introduced us. I stepped forward to shake hands, but stepped back when I saw that Collins had made no similar move. 'Take a seat,' was all he said. 'On the floor. I've got all the available chairs. Be with you in a minute, when this race is finished.'

I sat on the floor, crossed my legs and lit a cigarette. Wentworth did likewise, looking at me with a strange weak grin, and then he turned away. Eventually, after a long period of silence, Collins put down the transistor radio and spoke to me.

'I backed the wrong horse,' he said. 'So what's *your* racket, mate?'

'My what?'

'What do you *do*?'

'I'm doing nothing in particular at the moment.'

'Then why move into this dump?'

'Because the taxi driver dropped me off here.'

'You got money?'

'Enough.'

'How'd you get it?'

'None of your damned business.'

'It might be.'

'I'm not used to being questioned by…'

He let the silence hang there, deliberately, his brown, unrevealing gaze never leaving my face. Then he finished the sentence for me: 'By an Abo?'

'By anyone.'

'You just said the right thing, white fella. You might not have meant it, but you said it. Maybe your

26

new friend here...' he nodded to indicate Jim Wentworth ... 'maybe he coached you beforehand.'

'Nobody coached me.'

'Glad to hear it. It reaffirms my faith in the goodness of human nature. Jim, get that bottle of Scotch out of the cupboard. Also three glasses. Let's all relax while I tell the new boy a few things.'

Wentworth jumped to his feet with an energy I hadn't expected to see in him. When he opened the cupboard door, I was amazed to see a wealth of various liquor bottles standing on shelves also littered with thick envelopes and cardboard boxes. Wentworth took down a bottle of Haig Dimple and three glasses, making me wonder if this was where he obtained his own booze. He poured three stiff shots and handed each of us a glass.

Collins hadn't moved from his outstretched position between the two armchairs. He looked kind of lordly lying there like that, being served by a suddenly obsequious Jim Wentworth. Collins had a mouthful of his Scotch, then he started talking.

'Firstly – just in case you're harbouring any snotty ideas about who you will and who you *won't* live with – I want you to get it through your head that this whole building is owned, not by the old bag who rented you the room, but by *me*. Understood?'

'Understood.'

'Good. No regrets?'

'No.'

'Even better. I'm beginning to feel heartened. You noticed the contents of that cupboard when Jim here fetched the booze?'

'I noticed. I'm impressed. You could open your own liquor store.'

'You curious?'

'What do you think?'

'I think that's a good answer. All right, white fella, here it is. The grog was paid for by the contents of the envelopes you saw. The envelopes contain photographs of a specific nature. The photos are sold illicitly by various aides of mine, including your new friend, Jim Wentworth. You see, Jim drinks twenty-four hours a day and I keep him supplied. Isn't that right, Jim?'

'That's right, Collins.'

I glanced at Jim. His face was turned down and away. He was drinking methodically from his large glass of Scotch.

'Jim's got nothing against Aborigines, nothing at all. Have you, Jim?'

'No, Collins, nothing at all.'

'Now, me, I've got plenty against the Aborigines. Just because I happen to be one of them – white fella for a dad, pure Abo for a mum – doesn't mean I'm prejudiced in their favour. Far as I'm concerned, if the bomb drops they can drop it on them as well – just as long as it doesn't get me.'

'Nice.'

'Well, as my old grandpappy said, before he died of malnutrition in the sticks, that's life.'

'Still nice.'

'You're a cute one, Mr. Andy White, real cute. So cute I'll let you stay on for now – as long as you continue to pay your rent.'

'Gee, thanks.'

'You intend *working* around here?'

'No.'

'You've got to pass the time *somehow*.'

'I'm a writer.'

'What have you published?'

'Nothing.'

'Then you're not a writer; you're a bum. And, if I may say so, you *look* like a bum.'

'You want comparisons?'

'Don't push me, white fella. I'm no bum. Black, yes – bum, no. You guys walk in here thinking you're hotshots and you all float out looking like damp rags. Me, I'm the Aboriginal you all secretly despise, but I'm also the owner and boss man of this dump, and anything you want, you get from me. For me, the honourable Jim Wentworth here sells dirty pictures and the little lady downstairs flogs her one and only talent. I was here when they floated in and I'll be here when they float out. As for self-deluding drifters like you – you all come here looking for something, and whatever it is – sex, excitement, cheap thrills or oblivion – I'm the man you have to buy it from. You may resent my presence, you may even hate it, but under these particular circumstances you can't afford to ignore it.'

'I'll just pay my rent, thanks.'

'That's the only relationship we need. You want another drink?'

'Sure.'

'It's only ten in the morning.'

'I'll chance it.'

'You haven't been off it much recently, have you?'

'I'll pay my rent.'

'And you'll write?'

'Yes.'

'How long have you been telling yourself that?'

'This time I mean it.'

'Sure, that's what they all say. Behind every neon light in the Cross there's a fella just like you – a small, scared, defeated thing crying that he doesn't belong here, that he's just passing through. Believe me, if they knew the truth, they'd shit themselves. But what they

29

say to themselves *is* true, in a sense. They often *do* just pass through – but they come in as half-baked humans and they leave like wet spaghetti. You know what I call them? I call them "the running men". And believe me, friend, you look like a running man.'

'I'm running from nothing.'

'Then why do you scream in the night?'

* * *

Across a short but potent distance we stared silently at one another – and I felt like murdering the black bastard. His gaze was cool, but his grin was mocking. It almost felt as if he had slapped my face. I'd never known any Aboriginals before and I hadn't thought about them one way or the other, but I sure as hell didn't like *this* icy character.

Once more, inexplicably, I recalled my father's dying words and this time they really shook me – so badly I felt myself sweating. A queer sort of panic built up in me, making me want to flee from the room. I was just about to do so when a low whistle sounded outside, seeming to come from Wentworth's room. Instantly, Wentworth jumped to his feet, a panicked look on his face.

'That's my sister,' he said, and abruptly left us.

Collins and I stared at one another.

'Tell me,' Collins said, running a finger around the rim of his glass and smiling slightly, maliciously, 'do you like being alive, Mr. White?'

'Yes.'

'Are you sure?'

'Yes.'

'That's what Wentworth says – from the bottom of a glass – but Wentworth, really, doesn't like being alive. Life frightens him because it's not as neat and clean as he'd like it to be. A sensitive fella. One day he started drinking and couldn't stop. Now, he never will. Fellas like him just haven't the nerve to top themselves. I'd say that Wentworth once lived as a guy carrying his illusions as a few extra layers of skin. Now he suffers the pain of having that protective skin torn from him.'

'You don't sound sympathetic.'

'You want I should weep? Listen, man, I *look* at life. I *see* it. When you know that your ancestors have been wiped out just like the American Indians, as sport for white men's guns, you learn to live with few illusions. They're out to kill me off, too, but they won't succeed. I've taken their own human flotsam, used it and abused it, surrounded myself with it, so now they can't reach me. As for sympathy: I can't afford that white fella's luxury.'

'It's cheap.'

'So is pain. Besides, Wentworth wouldn't accept my sympathy – and he wouldn't accept yours. You've heard him talk, haven't you? He mumbles and moans and he gives nothing back. Man, he is *terrified* of sympathy. From everyone, that is, except his sister. She comes here once a week, hoping to save him from himself. He waits for her like a child, yet always sends her away empty-handed. She wants him to go home with her. He's frightened to go home. All in all, a pretty unique situation.' He paused. 'You like women?'

'Pardon?'

'Don't bother replying. You've had a few troubles in that direction, haven't you?'

'A few, but minor.'

'Jim's sister's a real good-looker. A real *sweet* good-looker. But virtuous. Would you like to meet her?'

'Why do you offer?'

'Just a sociable gesture.'

31

'I doubt it.'

He laughed then. He threw back his head and laughed a long time: a rough-edged, bitter, admiring laugh. 'Man,' he said, 'you're a cool one. Sure, I've got a reason – but what's that to you? Do you want to meet her or don't you?'

'I'll meet her. Why not?'

He threw me a shrewd, calculating glance, then, swinging his short legs to the floor, he stood up and went to the door. I followed him out of the room and was led along the corridor to Wentworth's room. Wentworth sat on the bed, his face turned slightly to the wall, glass of Scotch in his hand. Sitting in a chair, facing him, her hands folded primly on her lap, a look of real anxiety on her face, was his sister.

She was the most stunning girl I had ever seen.

*   *   *

She was wearing a simple black sweater and dark green slacks. Her hair, also dark, matched her eyes and was piled high on her head. It was the sort of hair that instantly made me think of the clashing whiteness of a pillowcase in the night. Though possibly too thin, her breasts were full, her legs long. When Collins and I entered the room, she looked up with those dark, anxious eyes. Collins was grinning in a manner I didn't like.

'Morning, Miss Wentworth.'

'Oh,' she said, her voice flat. 'You.'

'The man himself.'

'I don't need your help.'

'I didn't offer it.'

Taking her eyes off Collins, she glanced in a cursory manner at me, then looked back at her brother. He was seated on the side of the bed, his shoulders hunched, the glass of Scotch being twisted nervously in both hands. He did not return her stare; he was looking down at his glass. I recalled him saying of his own appearance: 'In the daylight I look it.' Now I knew what he had meant.

'Jim, come with me,' his sister pleaded.

'No.'

'Please.'

'No.'

'You'll have to face them *sometime*.'

'I can't.'

His tone of voice shocked me. This wasn't the sardonic, elliptical way of talking that I'd heard before: this was the broken voice of a craven thing. Not for me, pal, I thought. Not for me. The girl was now looking harshly at the maliciously-grinning Collins.

'Why don't you throw him out?' she demanded. 'Why don't you throw him out so that he *has* to come home?'

'He pays his rent.'

'Throw him out and *I'll* pay his rent.'

'Laura, stop this,' Wentworth said.

'Well?' Laura asked of Collins, ignoring her brother.

'Can't do,' Collins said.

'Why?'

'Why should I?'

I admired the way in which she stared directly at Collins, her gaze hard, bright and dangerous, her expression both haughty and challenging. I realised, then, that Wentworth came from a reasonably wealthy family.

'To save his life,' she said.

'It's his life,' Collins responded.

'You're full of hate, aren't you?'

'That's *my* life.'

'Laura,' Jim mumbled, sounding distraught, 'please… stop this…'

'He likes it,' Collins said, grinning at me as he nodded in the direction of the young old man. 'He really likes this weekly beating. He's not only a drunkard but a damned masochist as well. Every time she comes to see him, he begs her to leave off, leave him alone, but if she missed coming some week, he'd fall to pieces. He likes being whipped by Florence Nightingale.'

'You shut up!' Jim suddenly screamed. 'You leave off calling her names like that!'

'Be quiet, Jim,' Laura said, patting him gently on the shoulder while still looking directly at Collins. 'Calm down.' She took her hand away from her brother's shoulder. She kept her eyes on Collins. For a brief moment there was an uneasy silence. When finally Laura spoke again, her voice was flat, resigned, despairing.

'I know why you like having him here,' she said. 'I know,' she repeated, speaking softly, almost whispering, and nodding her head as if to herself. 'You want to destroy him, don't you? You want to watch him commit suicide… and you want to help him do it. Isn't that true, Mr. Collins?'

'Isn't that a touch dramatic, Miss Wentworth?'

'Get out,' she said, still speaking softly.

Collins didn't move. She looked up, saw the mocking grin on his face, and then, suddenly, something exploded inside her, sending her to her feet with fists clenched, her body quivering in front of Collins with a shocking, almost insane, rage. 'Get out! Get out! *Get out*!' she shrieked.

Collins grinned, bowed politely, and we left.

Chapter Three

THE CROSS

'You want to see the Cross?'

'Yes.'

I wanted to get out of that place, at least for a few hours, and I wanted another drink. Though I recalled my many resolutions about not drinking, I still wanted a drink. How could I settle down in a menagerie like that? Especially after what had just happened. It was impossible. Besides, I hadn't slept all night and the last week had been rough. *You're a wastrel…* No, but I was sick. No two ways about it. Sick in the gut. The thing to do was relax this day. By tomorrow I'd be fit again and raring to go.

So I left the rooming house with Collins. He walked confidently beside me, a tight grin on his face. Thinking of what he'd said to me, to Jim Wentworth, and to Wentworth's sister, I couldn't help but come to the conclusion that he was the biggest bastard in my experience. Yet I had a sneaky admiration for him. For some reason or other I had taken to him. He made me think of a rock isolated in a stormy sea, forever pounded by the waves yet never moving, relishing its punishment. Possibly that's what I most liked about him: he looked as if he had the strength to endure.

*   *   *

It was just past noon and as we entered the Red Light district of Kings Cross, known locally as 'the Cross', I had a good look around me. The place was crammed with shops, restaurants, pubs, strip clubs, hotels, brothels, pedestrians and dense, noisy traffic. It was certainly a busy area. It had atmosphere. The place was alive with the promise of pleasures to come, particularly in the evening. And I was certainly looking forward to the evening.

'You hungry?' Collins asked.

'Moderately.'

'Then let's eat.'

We turned into Roslyn Street and went down a single flight of stairs into a semi-dark restaurant. The place was crowded, mostly with young people, some in their teens, others about my age, drinking coffees or having lunch while Italian music played softly in the background. More middle-class than bohemian, though Collins seemed perfectly at home here and clearly knew the staff. He didn't ask me what I wanted. He just ordered spaghetti bolognese and black coffee for two. He didn't speak until he had finished eating, then he leaned back casually in his chair, lit a cigarette, and said, 'That sister of his... She sure is some looker, isn't she?'

'She's okay.'

'Don't act casual with me, White. I saw your eyes when you were peeping.'

It was true. The minute I'd seen her, I'd fancied her.

'She's a looker,' I conceded.

'She's also his greatest weakness.'

'Come again?'

'He's crazy about her. I mean, really *crazy* about her. Let me clue you in on our friend, Jim. He's an idealist, a dreamer, a fella who imagines himself so sensitive, he can't look at this dirty old world without feeling revolted. It's not an unusual disease with your breed. Some people, if they haven't got real problems, have to invent them. So it is with Jim. He's a poetic soul who's afraid to face the crude realities of life on this foul earth. He sees corruption wherever he looks and he can't bring himself to live with it. The only pure thing left on his horizon is his sister. Man, for him she's the virgin angel! When she comes to see him, the sun comes up. It's a rare kind of love... So rare, it's destined to be destroyed.'

'How do you mean?'

'You didn't eat much,' he replied.

'We weren't talking about my food.'

'That's what I like about you, White. For a running man, you're unusually direct.'

'I'm not a running man, whatever that is.'

'Running men? They're a breed apart and they never stop moving. They run fast, they run scared, and they're perfectly legal. They just can't face reality. Now me, I don't have a choice. I've *got* to face it.'

'Why do you live... like you live?'

'And how do I live, man? Define it for me.'

'In the gutter.'

He just grinned. 'That's right, white fella,' he said, 'in the gutter. Just remember, there's such a thing as unofficial allocation: born an Abo, allocated to the gutter, by popular consent, without votes. Man, I have no place else to go.'

'You could do better.'

'Could I? Could I *really*? You know, that's what I most like about you white Aussies – your sublime innocence about guys like me. Man, they do not exactly reserve the *cream* of opportunities for we Aboriginal masterminds. Not even for a sweet fella like me.'

'I think if you're smart enough, you can make out okay.'

'Well, listen. Some of my most intelligent friends are those winos you see slurping methylated spirits down on the 'Loo wharves. I'd probably be in the same boat except that I have steel in my brain and a little ice in this fighting heart and I don't like the white fella's boot on the back of my black neck. Jack Collins bows to no man. I'm a pimp, a pedlar of flesh and filth, but the one thing I *won't* be is a doormat for white men's feet.'

I didn't like conversations like this one. I didn't really understand what he was talking about and I didn't want to. I'd never said a word against the Aboriginals in my life, so I couldn't comprehend why he was telling me all this. Besides, it didn't seem to have much to do with what he had said to Jim Wentworth. For this reason, I said, 'That was still a bad thing you did to Jim in front of his sister.'

'Why? The fella's stewing in his miserable self-pity and I don't let him forget it. That's bad? Listen. Fellas like you and Jim haven't got a real problem in the world. It's just self-pity, self-delusion, and these are luxuries only you so-called liberal white Australians can accord.'

'So you'd like to destroy people like us.'

He drew on his cigarette, leaned back farther in his chair, smiled expansively and said, 'Yes.'

*   *   *

He had it in him. This I knew. I could see it in the hard bright flare of his eyes as he talked. I also saw it, later that evening, in the way he traversed the darkening but neon-lit streets of the Cross, a lithe, sardonic, unloved wanderer. He weaved through the crowds with the brash confidence of a man who expects trouble around every corner and knows he can handle it. On those rare occasions when he passed a fellow Aboriginal, he offered no glance of recognition or understanding. People looking at him were forced to look through him.

Yet eventually I had the peculiar feeling that their eyes were upon *me* – slyly, meanly, filled with condemnation and distaste.

By this time we had been drinking heavily for a solid nine hours. The pearly light of day had gradually faded into a technicoloured dream, the neon signs blending with the street lights and the headlights of many cars. I had the feeling that we'd been in and out of every bar in the Cross, and a few other besides. Collins had also taken me into some of the strip clubs where the chairs were stacked upside-down on most of the tables, the lights were still on because some drunks were still present, and the atmosphere, with its stale booze and cigarette smoke, was utter desolation. I didn't like the faces of the men I saw in those places. They were faces that told of bleak bedsits and grim dawns, the sort of faces that only come alive in degradation or violence. Most of the women, the strippers and whores, came into the same category, but Collins talked to them, casually, indifferently, giving nothing and expecting nothing in return. This was his world.

'Tell me,' he said at one point, 'just what do you intend writing about?'

'Whatever I see around me.'

'You won't stay anywhere long enough to really see *anything*.'

'I have and I will.'

'White, do you have friends? Relatives?'

'Yes.'

'And they consider you a failure?'

I hesitated, then: 'Yes.'

Too late, I realised that once more my noble resolutions had flown, like a bird, right out the first bar window. During the preceding long night I had sworn to lay off the grog, to discipline myself, to work, and I had determined to do it because I was frightened – yes, frightened of something that wouldn't fully come into focus in my thoughts. I hadn't wanted to get drunk again, but I *was* drunk – and I knew that I was drunk because Collins had planned it that way. Already he had wrung from me a confession I hadn't wanted to make.

When, again, I began to recall my father's parting words, I reached for the latest drink as if for oblivion. And that's when I sensed, though could not define, the trap.

'How did you actually fail, White?' he asked.

'I didn't actually fail.'

'What *did* you actually do?'

'Nothing serious.'

'Go on.'

'Not much different from a lot of other fellas my age. For one thing, I liked the girls too much. Always in trouble with the girls. The last being the worst. Unwanted pregnancy, irate parents, the works. My own parents were well fixed financially, so they dealt with the situation and I was merely reprimanded, frowned upon, temporarily excused, though it didn't help much. I meant to change, I really *wanted* to change, but… things just happened… Then I was thrown out of university. When my dad expressed his outrage, I confessed that I wanted to be a writer. Though disgusted, describing it as just another of my many impractical notions, he gave me the money for a trip overseas, telling me to go off and work it out, give it a go, but all I did was get into more trouble and wire him for the money to get me home. I kept trying to write, kept trying, but never seemed to have enough time, always out on the town, the relentless social binging, until the day my dad called me into his study for what he said was a final talk. I started to abuse him. We ended up screaming at one another. That's when he had the first of his heart attacks. It was just old age. I'm sure that's all it was. But my mum and sister blamed me – and so did he. The day before he kicked the bucket, he called me into his bedroom, to his sick bed, and bluntly disowned me. Raving. When he died, I got the hell out of there.'

The instant I stopped talking, I regretted what I had said. I shouldn't have told Collins so much about myself. I knew that for sure. Collins looked at me with oddly sleepy, veiled eyes and what may, or may not, have been a smile. Then he said softly, slowly, clearly: 'I could almost swear that you and Jim Wentworth are one and the same.'

'Shut up, Collins.'

'Amen,' he said.

*   *   *

It was a large, dreary room with two single beds pushed against opposite walls and a dusty lime-green curtain that could be pulled across as a divider. I sat on the edge of one of the beds with a glass of whisky in my shaky right hand and my weepy eyes fixed on the bare floorboards. The night had been a long time in passing and the morning's early hours weighed heavily upon me. We had floated along on a river of booze and conflicting talk and now here I was, slap-bang at the unavoidable crossroads of a neon-coloured dream.

Lying back on the other bed, legs crossed, head propped up on a filthy pillow, a glass of whisky in his hand and a grin on his dark face, was the seemingly inexhaustible Jack Collins. By now I was starting to think of him as some kind of devouring spider, with myself, Jim Wentworth and Jim's sister trapped in his web.

'When are they coming?' I asked.

'Soon,' he crooned. 'Soon.'

'I didn't want to get this drunk,' I said, hearing my own voice as if from a great distance.

'Didn't you?' he responded with a grin that somehow unnerved me.

'You planned it.'

'Did I?'

'Yes.'

'And for why would I plan it, Mr. White?'

'I don't know.'

'The whores. Naturally you didn't want the whores either.'

'I'll have one.'

'In order to blame me tomorrow?'

'I don't know what you mean.'

'I didn't chain you to a glass, I'm not about to chain you to this room. You may leave, if you wish.'

'I'm not leaving. So?'

'Well, it seems to me that certain people won't make decisions for themselves, in order that others can be blamed for the decisions made for them. I mean, here I am, practically a stranger to you, yet already shouldering the blame for your drunkenness. An interesting turn of events, yes? When you wake up tomorrow morning, with a thick head and bloodshot eyes, unable to even look at your precious typewriter, let alone use it, will you blame me for that well?'

'No.'

'When you face the wall, will you face yourself?'

'I don't know what you're talking about. I'm having a night out on the grog and the women – all perfectly normal, the everyday thing. Why, then, the big spiel?'

'Because, my friend, you're not going to *stop* having nights out. Because you floated in here on a bottle of booze and you'll float out of here the same way. Because your eyes only open wide when your back's turned to whatever it is you're supposed to be looking at. And why? Because you're a running man and it's too late to stop.'

'Shut up.'

'One thing I'd like. I'd like you to get Wentworth's sister. Naturally, being an Abo, *I* can't get her. But you… Well, I think you could. And that I would like. That I would *really* like.'

'Why?'

'Here they come, man. I hear their footsteps.'

There was indeed a scuffling of feet on the landing outside, some soft female giggling, then the knocking of knuckles on the door. Collins told them to come in and they did, two already drunken whores with heavily made-up faces. I'd never been with women like this before and I didn't like being with them now. I felt somehow degraded. But I wasn't about to walk out, wasn't about to let that Abo bastard laugh in my face, so I hastily drained my glass, waved languidly at the two women, and gave as good a welcoming smile as I could manage.

'I see you brought another bottle, as requested,' Collins said to the peroxide blonde, grinning at her, not moving from where he lay.

'Lover, yes,' she responded, blinking heavily mascaraed eyes. A forty-year-old trying to be twenty. 'For you, anything goes.'

'That's what I like,' Collins said. 'A woman who does her master's bidding. Now top up our glasses and help yourselves.'

It was obvious that both women had been drinking most of the evening. Collins, I knew, had called them at some bar or other. 'That's where the trade is, man,' he had said with a crooked grin. 'They may get drunk, but at least they get paid. Also, it's convenient. If drunk enough, their clients often end up in an alleyway, beaten unconscious and robbed of their wallets. So be prepared: don't expect a pair of beauties, just a couple of pretty average females.' Looking at the two giggling women, I knew what he meant. The peroxide blonde had already topped up our glasses and was now filling two more glasses for herself and the full-bodied brunette. The latter, when she had a glass in her hand, came to sit beside me on the bed. She had a badly lined face disguised with a visible layer of pan make-up. She also had the natural appeal of an ageing woman who had once been attractive.

'Tut, tut,' she said, making fun of me. 'Lover-boy looks lonesome.'

'Lover-boy is fine.'

'You're quite a looker, sweetheart,' she said. 'If a bit on the worn side.'

'The pressures of the day.'

She arched a painted eyebrow. 'My! Jack here must have been showing you a thing or two.'

Collins interjected. 'Jack has done nothing but talk and drink all day. Of all else, he is innocent.'

'Jack,' she retorted, 'was never innocent. Not since the day he was born.' She placed a heavy hand on my thigh, ran it down the trouser leg to the knee, smiled with surprising sweetness, and asked, 'What's your name, darlin'?'

'Andy.'

'A fried kipper, are you?'

'Pardon?'

'English.'

'Yes.'

'A pom.'

'An immigrant a long time ago. I came here as a five-year-old with my parents.'

'Nothing wrong with that, darlin'. We welcome all to the land of milk and honey. So why do you look so grim?'

'Not grim,' Collins said from across the room. 'Just the sensitive type.'

The blonde staggered drunkenly across the room to sit on the edge of Collins' bed, placing one hand on his thigh.

'Don't crease the pants,' he said in that crooning, almost menacing, tone of voice. 'These pants cost me good money. When I want your hands on me, I'll tell you.'

Instantly, as if slapped on the face, the blonde withdrew her hand, shifted slightly away from him, and took a quick, nervous sip of her whisky.

'We having a party tonight, Jack?' the brunette asked.

'We just might,' he replied.

'Well, darlin',' the brunette said, turning back to me, 'if we're going to be together for a few hours, I might as well tell you my name. It's Leonie.'

'Leonie. That's a really nice name.'

She offered that surprisingly sweet smile. 'You're not so grim.'

Out of the corner of my eye, I saw Collins tugging the blonde down beside him. He didn't say a word. He just pulled her down. She placed his glass and her own on the bedside cabinet and stretched out beside him. It all seemed very slow, very dreamlike, the pale, dying ballet of a drunkard's hallucination. I wanted to say something – something important – but I couldn't think of what it was. Then, still holding her glass in one hand, Leonie slid both arms around my neck and, with the warm weight of her aged, asexual body, gently forced me backward onto the bed.

'Okay, Lover Boy,' she whispered, suddenly not sounding sweet at all. 'Let's play.'

For the first time since learning what it was all about, I found myself lying with a woman I didn't especially want. Something akin to terror shot through me, then instantly subsided. Her hand reached out to the small shelf at the head of the bed, slightly above it, and the glass scraped noisily on the wood. My arm dropped over the edge of the bed and I set my glass on the floor. I then fell completely backward with Leonie's body stretched across me. Out of the corner of my eye, I had a swift, startling vision of Collins and the blonde, both naked, writhing on their own bed. The bare bulb above us was blazing. *Not here*! I thought. *Not now*! The bolt of terror shot through me once more, then Leonie's arms were around me, her lips were clamped to mine, something screamed within and the real world was blotted out.

'Yes!' I gasped.

*   *   *

It was three in the morning when we left that room and walked the dark, chilly streets. The Cross was like a dead beast whose neon eyes had been gouged from their sockets, leaving only pools of impenetratable darkness. A few drunks and drug addicts still wandered about; a few whores stepped out of the shadows to whisper invitations. Overhead, the stars glistened in a velvety sky. Tattered newspapers rustled in the gutters, blown along them by a moaning wind. Footsteps ricocheted. Laughter reverberated distantly. I felt like scum.

'Alive!' Collins exclaimed excitedly. 'I feel alive! You want another drink, White?'

'No.'

'You may not want it, but you sure in hell need it. Brother, did you *perform*!'

I felt sick and guilty and degraded, my spirit numbed, my body exhausted. It had been an act of desperation, carried out in terror and unfathomable despair. The experience was new to me and one I hadn't relished. I had never been with a whore before, at least not a professional, and the event was not something I could be proud of. In the writhing, heaving shadows of the recollection was the rancid bite of true squalor. Once, in my drunkenness, I had thrown up over the side of the bed. We had all, the four of us, laughed and continued with what we were doing. And what I still couldn't forget was my glimpse of Collins' eyes, focused intently upon me as I writhed on the bed, at once mocking me and enjoying his victory over my failed hypocrisy. No, I could not forget that and felt sick to my soul.

'Don't act superior,' he now said.

'What?'

'Nothing. We're here.'

The Members Only club was in one of the narrow side streets off Darlinghurst Road. The neon lights had been turned off, the front door was locked. Collins stooped down and pressed a buzzer that was situated about six inches above the ground. He straightened up again as the door opened a little. A pale, gaunt face stared out at us, then the man said, 'Jack?'

'The man.'

'Jesus, don't you ever rest?'

47

'Don't see the point of it.'

There was the rattling of a chain, then the door was opened fully and we stepped inside. It was pretty dark in there. We were standing at the top of a flight of stairs that led down to thin beams of light emerging from both sides of a black curtain. Following the gaunt man, who was wearing a brown roll-neck pullover and grey slacks, not sophisticated at all, we went down the stairs, through the curtain that he held open for us, and stepped into the crowded, smoke-filled club. The many human faces were ghastly in pale-green lighting, men and women still drinking and making a lot of noise. This riot of conversation clashed with the wailing jazz combo on a postage-stamp stage. In front of the band, a young woman was performing a striptease, slowly, rhythmically, as if in a trance. Collins and I took a table towards the back of the club. Collins ordered double Scotches for both of us, then we stared silently at each other. I couldn't decide whether I admired or despised the lazily mocking grin he was giving me.

'Well,' he said finally, when the drinks had arrived, 'I'm sure giving you enough to write about.'

'For which I am humbly grateful.'

'And disgusted.'

'If you must know – yes.'

'You weren't chained. Remember that.'

'I didn't know it would be like that.'

'Cry innocence.'

'You tricked me.'

He looked thoughtfully at me for a few seconds, then, slowly, he leaned across the table, closer to me, as if in a conspiracy. His eyes were unusually bright, not bloodshot at all, flaring defiantly out of that dark skin, but it wasn't this that made me realise he was definitely drunk, despite his appearance to the contrary. It was the expression on his face: an expression of passionate, naked candour, of honesty bared like a bleached bone, of pain stripped to its final, essential nerve. It was the face of a man clinging to a precipice.

'You better listen and listen good,' he said, 'because I'm drunk now and I won't ever explain this again. You asked me if I'd enjoy destroying a man like Jim Wentworth and I answered *yes* and I meant it. I'd enjoy destroying him because only in that way do I find the means to live. You see, I can't *afford* weakness. I *will* destroy the sensitive Jim Wentworth and when I do, he won't have been the first and he certainly won't be the last.

'You think I despise Jim? Well, you're wrong. I despise what he's doing to himself – I despise that on principle – but I also love that kid because he has a genuine respect for me – and that's something I've found in few others. But I can't afford that kind of weakness. You understand? I love that boy and this is my weakness, so I have to kill it, to amputate it, otherwise I can't preserve the ice that I need in order to exist as I do.

'Perverse? Yes, to your way of thinking it might be. But what you've seen and experienced these past hours is the rotten underbelly of so-called civilised society – and this is all your white world has given me. To exist in it, I can't indulge myself in such luxuries as binding love or even friendship. The minute I open myself to these, I throw away my only line of defence. Strength is all that matters, steel in the soul, and a man can only temper this by cutting down all that he wants to love or respect, by leaving no open wound into which salt might be rubbed.'

He leaned back in his chair, lit a cigarette, puffed smoke to the already smoke-filled atmosphere.

49

'Look at you,' he said, with the greatest contempt. 'You sit there with your grim, sanctimonious, white man's face and your weak, blind, white man's eyes and you despise me for what I've shown you tonight. Tomorrow you'll say that you're only guilty by default, because only in this coward's manner can you experience what you want to experience. Like most of your privileged, self-absorbed young white brothers, you stumble carelessly through life with your eyes averted and throw your guilt onto the nearest living, breathing coat hanger: a family member or friend. Finally, you bury yourselves in a bottle, in a journey that doesn't end, or in a marriage that torments you into an early grave – and you do this saying, "I'm not guilty" or "I'm only guilty by default" or "Who am I to fight a cruel world?". And through all of this you still have the insolence to feel superior to Aboriginal trash like me who find our self-esteem in the gutter. Well, how fast do you run, Andy White? And once you've finished with your pious laments about my evil doings toward Jim Wentworth, how quickly will you forget his existence? If I accelerate his pain into his destruction, will you prevent it?'

I didn't reply. His words no longer meant anything to me. I felt sick, wretched; I wanted to crawl into bed and forget the whole sordid business. Pushing my empty glass aside, I looked down at the table, rested my forehead in my clasped hands, and said, 'Let's get the hell out of here.'

'You didn't disappoint me,' Collins said. 'No. You sure didn't disappoint me, white fella.'

*   *   *

We started along the dark, narrow street, saying nothing, temporarily tired of one another, possibly hating each other. Some other customers had tumbled out of the club with us and I could hear them close behind, laughing and yelling. Then one of them, deliberately louder than the rest, shouted out, 'Hey, mates, don't tell me we were drinking with an Abo! With one of those black bastards!'

Collins froze where he stood, his back still turned to the men.

'Looks like it, Charlie,' another man said. 'A genuine caveman. A boong.'

'Yeah,' the first man added. 'Let's throw another boong on the barbie.'

Still, Collins didn't move. The men behind us had stopped advancing when Collins stopped. Now no one was moving.

'Hey, can he talk?' another voice chimed in.

'Doesn't sound like it. Bet he can grunt, though.'

Collins stood his ground, looking straight ahead, not even bothering to turn around and face them. I had walked on ahead slightly; now I turned back to look at Collins and his antagonists. There were three men, all clearly drunk and dishevelled. In the moonlight I could see the crazy grins on their faces. They had inched forward a little and were now close to Collins, spreading out to form a semi-circle around him. One of them had a bottle in his hand.

'Hey, Charlie! Mind that bottle! Don't waste it on that boong bastard's skull!'

'Bloody oath, Charlie. What'll we play?'

'A game of football, fellas. With this coon's black head. You want to be our football, Blackie? Psss! Psss!'

Charlie and his mate kept inching forward, but their silent companion was slightly ahead of them. Encouraged by the taunts of the other two, he stepped up to about three feet behind Collins and snapped his fingers at the back of Collins' neck. 'Psss! Psss!' he hissed, as if calling a cat.

Hand slipping to his hip pocket, body dropping instinctively into a fighter's crouch, Collins spun around on the ball of one foot. There was a sharp clicking sound and then the flick-knife glittered in the moonlight, small, sharp and deadly. His antagonist jumped backward as the knife was waved to and fro in the air like a snake's head. Collins remained crouched low, his right arm slightly bent and outstretched, his thumb along the back of the blade. He was clearly no amateur.

'You want to play games, cobbers?' he whispered, coaxing them towards him with his free hand. 'You want to play with this black ape?'

'Why, you – '

There was the sound of the bottle smashing against the nearest wall. Collins turned his head slightly towards that sound as two of the men nervously inched backward and the one called Charlie advanced upon him with the broken bottle in his hand, the jagged edge turned outward.

'Blackie,' Charlie said, his face ugly, 'I'm gonna cut you up.'

He swung with the broken bottle, but Collins was quickly under it and away to the side, untouched. Charlie cried out, a guttural sound, as the flick-knife slashed through the side of his coat and nicked his skin. He turned quickly and moved backward, keeping the jagged end of the bottle in front of him as Collins advanced. Collins was smiling in a frightening, demoniac manner, waving his weapon from side to side in a calm, even, experienced motion. He now had his back to the other two antagonists.

'Get him, fellas!' Charlie bawled, an edge of panic in his voice, though nothing happened. His two friends remained well behind him, just standing there as if paralysed.

Now alone, in a panic, Charlie swung wildly with the bottle, trying to cut Collins' face. But Collins' flick-knife flashed and was gone again, having slashed a neat line along the side of Charlie's face. Charlie yelped with pain and raised his free hand to his bloody face. In a hoarse, pathetic tone, he cried out, 'Get him, fellas! For Christ's sake! While his back's turned to you!'

One of them nervously started forward, but when Collins took a step towards him, the flick-knife glinting in the moonlight, the man backed away, calling out, 'You started it, Charlie, so don't blame us! Fuck it, I'm getting out of here before the Filth come.' Then he started off along the street in the opposite direction and was soon joined by his companion, leaving Charlie alone.

Charlie backed away from Collins, trying, with his free hand, to stem the blood flowing from his slashed cheek, the broken bottle in his other hand wavering indecisively. He could see Collins' flick-knife thrusting out of the darkness right in front of him.

'No,' he whimpered. 'Please, I…'

'*Collins*!' I shouted, but it was too late. The flick-knife had flashed. Charlie grunted and jerked slightly backward from the impact. Collins stepped away, withdrawing the flick-knife as he did so, letting Charlie fall sideways into the wall.

Then Charlie started weeping. It was a sick, broken, choked sound that came from the big man as he leaned against the wall, clutching his bloody belly in his already bloody hands. 'What have ya done?' he blubbered. 'For God's sake, what have ya – ?' He didn't finish the sentence. Instead, he bent over, as if about to vomit, weeping, choking, mumbling to himself. Then he collapsed, sinking slowly, onto the tarmac road.

We didn't stop to examine him. He was dead.

Chapter Four

CHILDREN OF NIGHT

I lay on my bed the rest of that morning and most of the day, my mind constantly tortured by thoughts of that stabbed man lying dead on the road. A voice inside me kept screaming, 'Run! Run!' but I just lay on, sweating, falling in and out of troubled sleep, waiting for the cops to come and claim me.

Late afternoon, Collins came in. There was a hard, unfriendly light in his eyes, a strange calm about him. With what seemed like contempt, he threw a newspaper onto my lap and said, 'It gets a small mention on page four. They haven't any clues and put it down to a drunken brawl. They're still investigating. I'm going to throw a party tonight.'

'What?'

'I'm going to have a party. Tonight. Here.'

'Is this a joke?'

'No joke, white fella. I want to celebrate my first killing.'

He was grinning, but there was something terribly wrong about that grin. His underlip quivered; his eyes were fiercely challenging. I found myself thinking of dynamite, primed to explode, the fuse already lit.

'You don't mean that,' I said. 'We have to tell the police.'

'Man, you're crazy.'

'We *have* to tell them! It was an accident. He came at you with a bottle. They'll put it down to self-defence.'

He leaned over, grabbed me by the collar of my shirt and violently shook me.

'We do *not* tell them!' he whispered. 'You understand? We do *not* tell them! The Filth around here don't appreciate coloured savages attacking their good white citizens with flick-knives – and that, precisely, is what I am, white fella, a coloured savage with a knife. So we keep our clams shut. *Shut tight!*'

He shook me some more, shaking his meaning into me, then he dropped me back onto the bed. I lay there, breathing heavily, frightened, just staring up at him. Then I said, 'I don't want to be involved.'

'No one ever does,' he retorted, 'when it's too late to back out.'

Then he left the room.

*   *   *

The party didn't take long to get going because a lot of the guests were already drunk or drugged when they arrived. It was a mixed party, but most of them were young, in their teens or early twenties, casual in dress, glib in speech, some of the boys with hair as long as the girls'. They all seemed to have poured into Collins' room at approximately the same time, glasses in their hands, cigarettes of tobacco or marijuana at their lips, a lot of excited words on their tongues.

'I think the hippies are a gas. I love the bangles and beads. Sure as fuck they're the hope for the New Age. I mean, even in *Time* they've finally been treated with respect. Which just goes to show how *serious* they are.'

'I drink to the hippies – those flowered and dreamy social parasites.'

'I drink to *Time* – the new teen hip rag.'

'I'll take Dylan over the Beatles any day. "Like a Rolling Stone" is a fucking masterpiece.'

'Mick Jagger's "Satisfaction" beats it hands down.'

'Sorry, mate, but you don't know your shite from shinola.'

At the far end of the packed room, partly lost in the sea of flushed faces and purple smoke, Collins was in histrionically animated conversation with a long-haired blonde – boy or girl, I couldn't tell which. I only knew that I was frightened – and that I couldn't take my eyes off Collins. Every so often he would catch my gaze and stare at me with a cold, hard, mocking semi-smile that made me wonder what was going on in his head. I *did* know that he thought more about the killing than he was going to let on to me. *Run*! *Run*! whispered that voice in my mind. But I remained in my corner, in hiding, and drank… and drank.

'Hi, Andy.'

To my surprise, it was Wentworth, a crooked grin on his face, a water look in his eyes. The hand holding a glass of Scotch was shaking and he looked even worse than he had the previous day. Indeed, he looked like he had aged ten years in twenty-four hours. No longer did he have that glib, sardonic self-confidence.

'Hi, Jim.'

'You look worried, Andy.'

'Do I?'

'Yes. Like a hooked fish.'

'Just tired.'

'But you slept most of the day.'

'What is this, Jim? The third degree?'

'Sorry. And I'd also like to apologise for my performance yesterday.'

'Forget it. I can barely remember it.'

'My sister… she's rather… strong-minded.'

'I gathered.'

'But she's not mean.'

'No, I didn't think so.'

He grinned crookedly again, then looked down at the floor. His feet were shuffling restlessly, nervously.

'She has this bug,' he said, 'about Jack Collins. She has the screwy notion that he's trying to… destroy me.' Here, he chuckled uneasily and shrugged his shoulders. 'Ridiculous,' he said. 'She's so dramatic. I guess… I suppose… it's because we're so fond of each other. Much, much too fond of each other. Know what I mean?'

'Yes.'

'I'm just a plain drunkard. I know it. I accept it. Collins has nothing to do with it.'

He raised his eyes to look desperately at me, as if for confirmation of his last remark.

'No,' I said. 'Of course not.'

But he knew I didn't mean it. 'Andy,' he said in a tentative manner, his voice sounding strained, 'I want you to do something for me. It may sound crazy, but it's important. It's really important.'

'What is it?'

He glanced furtively left and right, then, breathing deeply but moving quickly, he pressed a piece of paper into my hand. I opened it up and read it. It was a telephone number.

'It's my sister,' he said, looking highly uncomfortable. 'If anything happens… tonight… anything that looks… bad… please ring her, get her over here… *immediately*.'

I turned my face away briefly, wanting to avoid his haunted gaze. When I looked back, he was already gone, lost in the dense cigarette smoke of the packed, noisy room. Through the haze, I saw Collins' eyes.

*   *   *

By midnight the place was a riot. New guests kept
arriving, but no one seemed to be leaving and the room
was so crowded you could scarcely move. 'Timber!'
someone cried out as a drunken woman keeled over.
The record player was blaring out some form of weird,
psychodelic music and those dancing in a fixed
position, having no space in which to move, looked as
if they were in a trance. Couples were hotly clinging to
one another in chairs, on the landing, on Collins' bed
and even on the floor. A self-styled professor of hip
philosophy was giving some kind of lecture to the girl-
boys and boy-girls packed adoringly around him.
Another group of starry-eyed hippies were debating the
possibility of finding God through LSD because that's
what a lot of them were on. A surprisingly young
novelist with long hair and no shoes, standing right in
front of me, was insisting to his girlfriend that the worst
writer in history was Victor Hugo and the best was Jean
Genet. 'My own books,' he said, 'are tone poems to
myself; I'm not interested in who understands me.'
Sitting in a chair pushed tight against the wall, looking
decidedly disgruntled, was the hunchback, Fields. He
was repeatedly, deliberately, tripping people up with
his walking stick, though most were so drunk they
scarcely noticed. By then I was pretty drunk myself,
with everything around me seeming unnaturally bright
and unreal. A couple of teenage girls, both in miniskirts
and well stacked, came over to talk with me, but
receiving little response from me, they turned their
noses up and moved on. I just didn't feel like doing
anything. I had seen Jim Wentworth go into the
bathroom with one of the junkies, clearly intending to
get high. Jack Collins was still sitting in an armchair, a

glass in his hand and that dangerous grin on his face. He waved at me.

'Come over here, white fella!' he shouted. 'Join the conversation. You might find it amusing.'

They say that only women have intuition. I don't know why, but when I went over to join the men and women grouped around Collins, I felt as nervous as Wentworth had previously looked. Then I remembered the note he had handed to me, his sister's telephone number, and I wondered what it all meant.

Collins' eyes focused upon me, with an uncommonly bright, challenging light in them.

'We were discussing murder,' he said.

I felt a chill go through me.

'Hardly amusing,' I said.

'Grisly,' said a hippie-styled brunette, shivering melodramatically.

'Yeah,' Collins said. 'One of the fellas here just happened to mention that stabbing we read about in this morning's paper. He thinks that killing, even for self-defence, is a terrible thing – something that would haunt the killer for the rest of his life. I told him that I thought murder, like any other form of violence, could in some instances be a form of therapy. I mean, you're an intellectual, White. Didn't Dostoyevsky say something like that?'

'No. Not exactly like that.'

'Well, he *should* have said something like that.'

Collins grinned and everyone laughed.

'I think murder might haunt a man,' I said.

'What about war?'

'Killing in war is different.'

'What's different about fighting for your life on a battlefield or fighting for your life in a back street in Kings Cross?'

I said nothing.

'Or, to push it a bit further, what if the fella who did the stabbing needed to test his own courage? To do something that would normally terrify him?'

'You're talking through your hat, Collins.'

'Well, let me ask you another question. What if the killer was goaded into it? What if he'd been reduced to the stage where he had no will power left, where he could not make a move unless someone else, his Svengali, ordered him to do so? What then?'

I wondered just what Collins was driving at, because he seemed to be deliberately veering off the original point. Then I found out.

'I mean, let's conjure up a suitable situation. Take, for instance, say a drunk, a hopeless alcoholic. And try to visualise that this fella is an alcoholic because he has absolutely no control over himself, because he needs *someone* to dominate him at all times. Now, you take a guy like this – probably otherwise a perfectly nice fella – you take this fella and I say that his Svengali, the one he totally depends upon, could drive him to either self-immolation or murder. Piece of pie.'

'That's horrible,' said the same girl.

'It couldn't be done,' said the young man beside her.

'Couldn't it?' Collins asked rhetorically. 'I put it to you: some human beings are born to be spat upon. They not only want to be degraded; at times they can't exist without it.'

'Crap.'

'You think so? Okay, to prove my point I'll give you a perfect example.'

'*No!*' I heard myself shouting, because I knew what Collins meant. I knew what he was trying to do.

All eyes turned upon me. The record player had been turned off and the music replaced with tense silence. I felt foolish, embarrassed and terrified. Collins was staring at me, mockery in his grin, a coldly fierce violence in his eyes. And stepping out of the crowd, clearly as high as a kite from whatever he had taken in the bathroom, but with dread draining the blood from his face, was Jim Wentworth, soon to be the victim of the proceedings.

'Dance, Jim,' Collins said.

'Please, I…'

Wentworth's words trailed off, he looked pleadingly around the crowd, then his eyes came to rest on me. Those eyes were naked with his growing humiliation. Even from where I sat, I could see his whole body visibly shaking. He looked like an animal trapped in a corner, blinded by panic, cringing in his helplessness.

'Dance, Jim!'

I closed my eyes. Something was beating incessantly in my head, my skin burned. Like a child of the night I wanted to run away and hide. When I opened my eyes again, Jim had moved to the centre of a cleared space, directly in front of Collins. He had a bottle in one hand, an imbecilic grin on his pale face. There was no music. No one was talking. Slowly, shamefully, Jim began to dance, his head bowed, his arms hanging loosely by his sides.

'Faster, Jim! Faster for the people!'

Collins started clapping his hands, a sharp, cutting, incessant sound, and Jim instantly moved faster, his feet kicking at the air in ungainly, idiotic movements, his arms dangling as if they didn't belong to him. Light flashed on and off the empty bottle in his hand, flashing across the eyes of those watching, some stepping back to give him more space. The ghastly silence was broken only by Collins' handclapping, Jim's awkwardly dancing feet, and an occasional, possibly embarrassed, outburst of laughter from an onlooker.

'Dance, Jim! *Dance*!'

Faster he went, ever faster, while other hands took up the clapping, general laughter was unleashed, and the faces of the onlookers became more flushed and sweaty with self-conscious, shameful amusement.

'Faster, Jim! *Faster*!'

Round and round Jim went, in a spinning, dizzying circle, his breathing harsh and strangled, the clapping pounding in his ears to goad him on, the laughter beating on his temples to encourage him. The bottle flew from his hand, went sailing across the room, above the heads of the crowd, to shatter against the opposite wall. A cheer went up from the crowd, the hands clapping even more, until, with a sudden, animal screech, Jim was up on a table, his own hands clapping, his feet stomping and kicking wildly. All the faces were turned up to him, eyes wide with disbelief, while also showing mockery, admiration or shame. And at that moment, Jim threw his arms wide, threw his head back and laughed, a high, uncontrollable, lunatic's laugh. Then he staggered left and right, fell to his knees, struck bottles, glasses and plates with his head, and finally fell sideways off the table.

He lay there, still laughing uncontrollably, as the cheers went up.

I phoned his sister.

*   *   *

'Where *is* he?'

'Listen, Laura, he – '

'Where *is* he?'

I took her up the stairs, along a corridor filled with cigarette smoke and the overflow of guests from the party, turned left and entered Collins' packed room. By now the party was in full swing, with people all over the place, The Who screaming 'My Generation' from the record-player, partners too crammed in to dance, so just writhing together. To my despair, a fairly large group still surrounded the table upon which Jim Wentworth was again at play, his laughter coming out in desperate gasps, his body naked but for the pair of trousers he was just about to inch down over his thighs.

Laura stopped in the doorway, momentarily frozen, her eyes wide with shock and disbelief. Her clenched fists went up to her mouth, she shuddered in horror, then, with a cry of 'Stop it!', she hurried to the backs of the spectators, hammered at them with her fists, and fought her way through to the table. 'Stop it!' she shouted once more while grabbing at one of Jim's jogging legs.

He didn't recognise her. Pulling his leg away, he continued with his demented, humiliating dancing, that moronic grin still on his flushed face. 'Jim!' his sister screamed. '*Jim*!' Then she bent over the table, covered her face with her hands, and began to weep.

'Hey, sweetheart, you're putting a dampener on our fun!'

'Just a joke, baby!'

'This sheila's a regular little Ophelia!'

Collins had removed himself to a far corner, giving the spectators more space, a tight, controlled grin on his face, sweat on his forehead, that strange, frightening brightness in his eyes. He didn't move.

Forcing my way through the revellers, I grabbed Laura by the shoulders and tried to drag her away. She looked up at her brother as if in a daze, raised one hand to him in useless entreaty, then, slowly, as if uncomprehending, let me lead her away. I placed her on the bed in her brother's room, then I returned to the party. I didn't know if I was being extraordinarily calm or extraordinarily excited. What I *did* know is that I was drunk in a way I had never been before. Jack Collins still stood in that frozen attitude in the corner of the room. His glacial eyes were looking at me and through me. Not knowing what he was thinking, I walked up to him and said, 'You're a bastard.'

'That's me, white fella.'

I started turning away, but was stopped by his hand on my shoulder. When I turned back to face him, I could hardly bear to look in his eyes. I had seen the far side of the moon in those eyes.

'I feel nothing,' he said, spitting out the words like snake venom, but somehow anguished for all that. '*I feel nothing!*'

I left him there. Pushing my way through the onlookers packed around the table, I grabbed Jim by the ankle and said, 'Come on down, Jim.' His leg jerked in protest, but he couldn't dislodge my hand.

'Hey, let him go, Cobber,' a male voice said. 'You're spoiling the show.'

Suddenly exploding, hardly knowing what I was doing, I let go of Jim's ankle, spun around to face the bloke who had spoken, and punched him in the stomach. When he doubled up, I went for his face, chopping upwards under the bridge of his nose with the back of my clenched fist. The sound of splintering bone was followed by his cry of pain, then he was falling backward, away from me, into the arms of his companions, with blood spurting out of his broken nose. He didn't move again; just hung there in his friends' arms. I stood still for a few moments, waiting for him to revive and come at me again, but thankfully he made no such move. All was shocked silence. Jim was now on his knees on the table, his face dulled by exhaustion, saying nothing. I took him by the arm and repeated, 'Come on down, Jim.' Without a word, he did as he was told.

'I will not forget this.'

That was Collins.

*   *   *

When we lay Jim on his bed, his sister sat beside him. Jim fell asleep immediately. His sister's dark eyes were tear-stained. Her long black hair now hung down around her shoulders. She was wearing a lime-green blouse to match the slacks she had been wearing before. The skin on her face and neck was pale and inviting.

'He needs the sleep,' she said.

'I reckon.'

Gently, she picked up his right hand, let it rest limply in her own. For the first time I saw that his hands were badly scarred. His sister was also looking at the scars, a faraway expression on her face. Then, slowly, she brought the back of his hand up to meet her forehead and let it rest there for some time. It was a kind of salute. This strange, lovely young woman, bowed over the hand of her brother.

Eventually, sighing, she placed Jim's hand back on top of the blanket, then picked up her shoulder bag and withdrew a packet of cigarettes. She offered me one and I took it. When we were both smoking, I sat on the floor close to her feet, my back resting against the bedside cabinet. I looked up at her, but she wasn't looking at me. Her dark, haunted eyes were focused on the opposite wall. Her voice was as soft as a caress.

'He was going to be a concert pianist,' she said, then she chuckled, almost as if in self-contempt, before repeating forlornly, 'A pianist.'

'What happened?'

'The day after he won a scholarship to the Julliard School of Music, he went out with his girlfriend to celebrate. More than his girlfriend: his fiancée. They went to a nightclub and drank a lot. Then, instead of getting a taxi to take them back, he foolishly decided to drive. At that time, he wasn't used to hard liquor. There was a crash. His fiancée was killed outright. His hands were jammed between the steering wheel and the dashboard. All his fingers were broken. He could have still played when they were fixed – not as well as before, but he could have played – but he couldn't accept what he'd done to his fiancée, to himself, to his talent, and so he started to drink. Once started, he wasn't able to stop. Ashamed of himself, scarcely able to communicate with his mum and dad or me, he left home and ended up here. Then he became involved with Collins, practically became enslaved by him, and that led on from the drinking to the drugs. Collins deliberately feeds him both the drink and the drugs to increase his dependency. And ever since, I've been trying to persuade him to come home and get the help he needs. I always lose. Collins always wins.'

Outside the room, farther along the corridor, the noise of the party was continuing unabated, but in my room, shielded by the gloom between myself and the girl I was craving, the silence was more potent than words. Twin threads of cigarette smoke drifted out of her nostrils and spiralled dreamlike about her face.

'What'll you do now?' I asked.

She shrugged. 'I recently moved into a large flat in Manly, to get away from our parents, in the hope that if he knew he could share a place with only me, not them – they make him feel more ashamed than I do – he might be more agreeable to moving out of here. I picked Manly because of the beach, which I thought might be good for him. At least with fresh air and exercise. I'll take him there right now. Hope he stays. Not sure that he will, though.'

'I'll help you take him there.'

'Thanks.' She blinked and rubbed her tired eyes. 'Sorry, but I've forgotten your name.'

'Andy White. I remember yours.'

She smiled painfully. 'Yes, of course. It wasn't that long ago.'

We shook Jim awake. He was so weak, he could scarcely stand. Laura placed one of his arms around her shoulders and I took the other around mine. Together, we half-walked and half-dragged him from the room.

Out in the corridor, where the atmosphere was more subdued, the party dying off, couples were necking and whispering passionately and chuckling. A few of them looked curiously at us when we passed them. Just as we passed Collins' room, he emerged to stand silently in the doorway. His eyes flicked from Laura to me, then turned to Jim. Grinning, he disappeared back into his room.

'I hate him,' Laura said, then said no more.

She had parked her car just outside the rooming house. We sat Jim in the rear, I took the front passenger seat, then Laura drove off. Occasionally, Jim would mumble something incomprehensible. Laura and I did not speak. Once or twice, I glanced sideways at her face. The profile was lovely but remote, all emotion seemingly checked with an iron will. Yet I had the feeling that she was possibly on the verge of collapse. It seemed to take hours before we reached her apartment block in Manly, located in a side street not far from the sea, but once inside her flat, we managed to put Jim, still dressed, to bed. After staying with him in the bedroom for a decent period of time, Laura, satisfied that he was soundly sleeping, joined me in the living room.

'Coffee?' she asked.

'No, thanks.'

'I couldn't stand it myself.'

It was now two in the morning. Outside, the world was dead. When we'd first entered the apartment, Laura had turned on a stand-alone lamp and it now shed its soft, warm glow across the living room, illuminating her back, placing her features half in shadow. We stood facing each other, mere inches apart. My breath was choked in my throat, rendering me speechless. The pale marble of her skin was hazy, slightly unreal, seductive. I knew exactly what was going to happen. I had the odd feeling that I shouldn't let it happen. And yet I knew, with a sad, disturbing feeling of loss, that I was going to let it happen.

'I want to thank you…' she began. Then, with a helpless, bitter, surrendering sob, she was in my arms. Kissing her, caressing her, crooning inane words of love to her, I sank with her to the carpeted floor.

It had to happen that way.

Chapter Five

THE AFFAIR

It was the first genuine love affair I had ever known, an overwhelming consummation of joy and pain. We surrendered to each other in bewilderment and exaltation, torn between what we both wanted and what we also feared. There was reluctance on both sides, the unspoken awareness that what we were doing could have no good ending, yet we sank down together, locked in our mutual longing and need, moaning to one another the broken words of our desire and despair. A virgin, she cried out once, in pain, consent and loss, and then we knew that the seal was set, that we would have to see through to the bitter end what we had, in reluctance, begun.

In the darkness beneath me, I saw the glistening of her tears. This filled me with a fear I could not comprehend. With shame, I recalled the wasted years of my life and the wretched ending to which those years already seemed to have come. I recalled the face of my father in death and his last, muttered words of condemnation. *Running man. Running man.* 'No!' I silently cried out in protest as I buried my face in her breasts and stifled my pain. This time I would try. I *would* try!

'Why?' she asked. 'Why did we do it?'

'I don't know.'

'I don't love you,' she said.

'Nor me, you.'

She chuckled at that, a soft, slightly bitter, chuckle.

'Love with the proper stranger,' she said. 'I suppose that's how it usually goes. You spend all your best years holding back, saving it, waiting for the right man, the right time, and then, in a single moment of madness, with the proper stranger, you give it all away and regret thereafter.'

'Not quite like that.'

'You care?'

'In a way.'

'I need no lies.'

'I offer none.'

'Did you pity me? Was that it? You saw this forlorn, lonely, virginal girl, distraught because of her alcoholic, druggy brother, weeping in your arms, secretly yearning, and you fulfilled all her needs.'

'Stop that.'

'Such a joke. Such a hideous, monstrous joke.'

'*Stop it!*'

I blocked her words with my lips, crushed her body with mine, let the pain sweep over and away as a price to be paid for this brief moment of peace. Her arms came around me, clutching, demanding, as if in search of rescue, and then her soft moaning filled my ears to strip me bare. She laughed and wept alternately. I felt her desperation writhing between us, making me want to run and hide, always running, always. 'It's *not* like that!' I heard myself whispering, but she just chuckled again, punishing me, punishing herself, saying, 'Nothing matters but this. I don't care about anything else. Just fuck me. Love me!'

Her body flowed into the darkness, pale lines of flesh, of rapture and resistance, time dissolving into a pearly dawn. I thought of how I had come to this place, of steel tracks etching parallel lines across the Nullarbor Plain, taking me from the moment of my father's repudiation, carrying me to this new moment of tormenting truth. I thought of her brother, Jim, lying like a broken thing on that single bed in the next room and I knew that she was thinking of the same thing. She proved this for a fact when she asked, 'Why do they do it? What they did to him?'

'I don't know.'

'There's a lot you don't know.'

'I think he frightens them. I think that unusual sensitivity often frightens people not so sensitive. Contrary to what we tell each other, most of us lead fairly dirty lives. I think they fear him because he reminds them of something they've lost: a kind of innocence.'

'Jim's innocent?'

'He was.'

She was smoking. Exhaling a cloud of smoke, she distractedly watched it spiralling above her head. The grey light of dawn was beginning to filter out from between closed curtains.

'He must never know,' she said, 'about us. You see, corny as it may be, he actually *does* believe in my virtue. Since the accident that broke his fingers and robbed him of his talent, since he started the drinking and the drugs, he's sunk to levels he wouldn't previously have tolerated in himself. The drinking, the drugs, the dependence on men like Collins: that pimp, that dealer, that ruthless manipulator. Yes, I believe that since then Jim's been trying to kill himself, to at least deaden his pain, and the worse he becomes, the more he puts me up on a pedestal, someone representing everything he's lost. Maybe he needs to believe that something, or someone, truly virtuous still survives in his world.' She paused, turned her head to stare at me

72

with dark, honest, merciless eyes, then added: 'I think it would kill him if he found out about us.'

I had to look away.

*   *   *

I left as dawn had started lighting up the room. Her clothes were scattered all over the floor and she was still lying there on the sofa, naked, her head turned away from me. Between us was something we could neither understand nor surmount.

Just before I left, she said, 'I want to see you again.' The words hung like lead in the still air.

'When and where?' I asked.

'Not here,' she replied. 'Not ever again. When I want you, I'll come to you.'

We left it at that.

In the early morning, the Cross was like a tomb. Rain clouds hung low over the rooftops of the buildings, increasing the feeling of desolation between pavement and sky. Discarded newspapers rustled along the gutters; the bin men were already at work. Here on the pavement, a drunkard snoring in sleep, there in the snack bar a cop wearily having breakfast, the traffic increasing by the minute. I felt the oppression as a heavy weight on my shoulders; the light wind sounded ominous to my ears. Tension lay under the surface of tar and cement.

The wind being warm, what chilled me?

When I returned to the rooming house, Collins was sitting at the top of the stairs, legs outstretched, a bottle of beer in his hand. He didn't smile when he saw me. He didn't move. In the corridor, in the rooms with open doors, I could see exhausted celebrants stretched out on the floor, sleeping it off. The whole house felt like a morgue.

'You took a long time,' Collins said, his voice icily calm, 'to put him to bed.'

'Yes.'

'Is he coming back?'

'I don't think so.'

'I haven't lost.'

'I think so.'

His eyes were bloodshot but alert. I had managed to forget him and the man he had killed, but now, in remembering, my fear returned.

'Do you want me to leave?' I asked.

'No,' he said. 'Stay, white fella. I want you to stay.'

*   *   *

I couldn't figure Collins. I couldn't understand why he hadn't thrown me out. In the weeks to follow there would be little love lost between us. He never spoke again to me, nor I to him. Between us lay the damning, secret knowledge of a man, a stranger, dead from a knife wound, of which there was no more word in the newspapers, no sound from the police. Possibly put down as just another unsolved murder, the city, at this time, being full of them. So Collins and I would look at each other and the knowledge of the stabbing would be between us, binding us together even as we were kept apart with our mutual contempt. Yet even though I despised him for what he had done to Jim Wentworth, for what he had done in that dark street, I still could not help but feel a certain admiration for him. Around him, now, was a blank wall of silence; behind that silence, more violence was surely building. I could never walk past him without feeling the very real presence of enormous, if corrupted, dignity. I also had the feeling that he was planning something… something dangerous… something destructive. This added to my fear.

And Jim Wentworth had finally given in.

*   *   *

For weeks he lay on his bed in his sister's apartment in Manly, moving only to go to the bathroom or to prepare some food for himself. When he wasn't thus engaged, he was lying on his back in order to stare blankly at the ceiling, the opposite wall or the floor. After a while, he began to look out of the window, at the pedestrians in the street below, at the traffic, at the small strip of beach visible beyond the rooftops. He talked little and he didn't read. Occasionally, he smiled. For the first time in years, he had stopped drinking and was getting no drugs.

'He's coming around,' Laura told me. 'I think he's really getting better.'

I didn't see him at this time, but Laura kept me informed, talking about him even when we made love, as if to punish us both.

'Yesterday, he actually went out walking. He went down to the beach.'

'That's a good sign,' I said.

'He'll improve as long as he's left alone. He mustn't know about us.'

'It might not bother him. He might even be pleased.'

'He wouldn't be pleased to know that his sister's being fucked by his friend.'

'Correction: being loved by his friend.'

'I love my brother – not you.'

'Just how much do you love him?'

'It's not incestuous, if that's what you mean. We're just unusually close because we were locked out by our parents. They were decent, but cold.'

75

'I had problems with my dad,' I said, 'so Jim and I might have something in common.'

'Don't you dare go and see him,' she said. 'If you do, you won't see me again.'

'We're not betraying him,' I said.

'Aren't we?'

'No.'

'Then stop worrying about it.'

She would come to visit me in the evenings, reluctance in her walk, need in her face, bitterness in her voice, having to pass a cynically grinning Collins who rarely budged from his watchful position in the doorway of his open room. They never spoke to each other, but between them was an antagonism requiring no words. Up the creaking stairs, along the grim corridor, past a mocking, mute Aboriginal male, into my room and my embrace.

'Why here?' I asked. 'Why do you insist on making love *here*?'

'Why not here?'

'It's no place for you.'

'Surprise. The man thinks I'm worth more!'

'Stop it.'

'Me? Your mistress? Your *whore*?'

'*Stop it*!'

She whipped me in order to whip herself. Coming to me out of her need, despising herself because of that need. The complexity of this female reasoning wasn't new to me; the intensity with which she suffered it was. Our love affair was, at first, moved by the always present threat of betrayal, of possible dishonesty on both sides, with tension always lurking under the surface, a formless, indefinable fear never far removed, her need to shame us both dominating all. She had a talent for mild emotional savagery, a tongue that cut deep and sharp with salt rubbed into the wounds. Sometimes I hated her to the degree where I wished to murder her; invariably, when she had left me, returning to her brother, I was stricken with a devastating sense of loss. I wanted her and I wanted her badly – this I knew. What I detested facing was the certain knowledge that this time the relationship was more than physical. Love, for me, had always been a romantic myth; I now refused to accept that what I was experiencing was just that. Yet, if it wasn't genuine love, just what the hell was it?

'How many women have you had?' she asked.

'None of your business.'

'Put me down in your little black book. Conquest number fifty-five, always begging for more. Your greatest achievement.'

'Why vomit on yourself?'

'Why not?'

This form of self-deflation, at which she was so adept, always succeeded in making me feel as cheap as she made herself out to be. I couldn't tell whether or not it was a deliberate ploy, but I always tried to fight back, desperately, hopelessly, not really understanding what I was fighting. As a mean of escaping, I tried my typewriter, but it never worked. When she entered my room, that bleak room with the single bed, I would turn away from the typewriter and the blank sheet of paper, to say, as harshly as possible, 'Take off your clothes.'

'Such enthusiasm!'

With those two mocking words, my face would be slapped. Then, with her eyes never wavering from mine, she would obey, her clothes dropping to the floor in a manner calculated to make them seem like vermin from the body of a corpse. Insulted, but still wanting her, I would throw her back onto the bed, expecting coldness, resistance, anything except the passion with which she would receive me. This was, inevitably, her final and most brutal note of mockery.

'Let's get out of here. For at least once, let's get out of this awful dump and into the light of day. See the city, go for a ferry ride, anything to get out of here.'

'I like it here,' she said.

'You loathe it here. You loathe walking up those stairs, you loathe walking past Collins, you loathe the sight of this claustrophobic, dusty room, you clearly loathe it all.'

'That's why I like it.'

'Oh, yes?'

'I like to go slumming.'

'We *could* be good for each other.'

'I won't let it happen.'

'Why not?'

'I won't be broken when it ends.'

'It doesn't have to end.'

'In the end, you'll run away.'

'Have you been talking to Jack Collins?'

'No.'

'To your brother?'

'No.'

'Damn you. Go fuck yourself.'

One day I dared to look into the small wall-mirror above the wash basin, trying to discern what it was that others saw in my face, that sign of moral cowardice, but I saw nothing other than bland and faintly dissipated good looks. Then the room door clicked open and she was laughing before I could step away.

'Oh, little boy blue, what can he do, to keep the devil away?'

It wasn't revenge that I found in our shared bed. In this, also, she had me defeated.

'You see, sweetheart,' she whispered, 'I want it.'

The promiscuity of my former life had led me to the stage where I no longer knew if it was pride or love that tied me to her. Blessed or cursed with good looks and a winning smile, I'd never had a girl walk out on me. Always, I had been the one who dropped them, the one who ran, and so, lying beside this dark-eyed mystery, seduced by the pale, flowing languor of her naked body, I came, for the first time, to the realisation of this fact. It drilled down deep and twisted inside me. Putting aside the pitiful remains of my pride, I thought, *I love her, I do*. But looking into the ambiguity of her gaze, I could not finally bring myself to say it.

Once more, when she was gone, when I slept alone, I dreamed of my father's open grave. Such dreams became intermingled with nightmares of that stabbed man bleeding to death in a dark street. I often screamed myself awake.

Finally, Jack Collins spoke to me.

'Man,' he said from his chair in the open doorway of his room, 'that little room of yours sure is busy lately.'

'You don't like it, ask me to leave.'

'No,' he said, 'I'm happy for you to stay. I'm a sucker for love.'

The tension mounted. I took to sitting in my room, biting my knuckles, waiting for the sound of her footsteps coming up the stairs and imagining that moment when she would walk past the mocking gaze of Jack Collins. I wondered what that dark, dangerous intelligence was planning and when he would spring whatever trap he was setting. Such thoughts really unnerved me. I knew that the wisest course of action on my part would be to move out, but as this would be the same as running away again, I just sat there in my room, day in, day out, listening for the diurnal sound of Laura's approaching footsteps.

'Today,' she said, 'Jim went out walking again. He came back sober.'

Following this, her talk about her brother intensified. For the first time I began to understand the true depth of her love for him. It also came to me that the embodiment of purity he had sought in her was merely a mirror to the feelings she had for him. To me, their relationship was an emotional jigsaw whose pieces were just beginning to fit together. Together they were walking an idealistic tightrope from which, sooner or later, one of them would have to fall.

'It's unnatural,' I said.

'What is?'

'Your relationship with your brother.'

'We grew up together. We were unusually close. Our parents were well off but remote, travelling a lot, never showing us affection, and we clung to each other for comfort. There's no more to it than that.'

'You thought Jim was a genius. You were in awe of his musical talent. You thought his talent made him someone special. Someone out of this world.'

'He lived for his music. He had no other reason for being. That made him a pure being to me.'

'Complete purity doesn't exist.'

'It did – once upon a time. Before the accident destroyed his talent and led to his need for self-destruction. Now, I just want to protect him.'

'Then let him grow up.'

'How?'

'By telling him the truth about us.'

'What truth? That his sister is sleeping with a man she doesn't give a damn about?'

'I don't think that's quite accurate.'

'Are you fishing for a little love?'

'Shut up, Laura. Just shut your mouth. I can't take any more of this.'

I couldn't sleep. I couldn't eat. I couldn't concentrate enough to write. The silent typewriter mocked me, as did Laura and my father's final words and the eyes of Jack Collins each time I had to pass him in the corridor.

No longer able to tolerate my room when left alone in it, I began, more and more, to go out when I knew Laura wasn't coming. The Cross and I became intimate. I walked the streets like a man lost in a desert and desperately searching for water. I had managed to stop drinking, had been dry for nearly a month, but now I hit the bottle again. Was this a sign that what everyone said about me was true? Back to the bottle in the face of every problem? Hell, no! It was just a drink or two, for God's sake! To prove this point, I stopped drinking for a short period and went to a lot of movies instead. On the silver screen I saw film stars solving all their problems with relative ease, but watching them didn't help me any, so I gave up on the movies and was reinstated with the bottle.

Around me flowed the countless pale or suntanned faces of the general public, their voices raised against the traffic, moving quickly and seemingly with purpose, looking like tomorrow didn't matter, and I wondered how the hell they managed to get out of their beds in the morning without screaming in protest. As I hurried towards nowhere in particular, I thought of Laura and Jim Wentworth, of the scheming Jack Collins, of the many tensions between us that were tearing me apart, and I hated the world, I cursed the world, and was filled with a restlessness that was all too uncomfortably familiar.

I won't run! I thought repeatedly, but I kept walking, if not running, just walking, walking, and it was during one such walk, around the El Alamein fountain in the heart of the Cross, that I ran into a healthier-looking Jim Wentworth. He blushed, glanced nervously around him, then punched my arm in a matey fashion and said, 'Let's have a coffee.'

*   *   *

There was little colour in his cheeks, but his eyes were clear and the old man's lines had disappeared. It was an improvement. He smoked a cigarette, fiddled distractedly with a spoon, and began, 'Listen, Andy, I want to thank you for – '

'Don't.'

'Yeah, well…'

'You're looking a lot better, Jim.'

'Well, mate, I *feel* a lot better. Haven't had a drink since that last… night… and had a damned good rest into the bargain. Walking a lot. Going to the beach a lot. Took me a long time to really come to my senses, but… Well, Laura, she sort of kept me a prisoner for my own good and now I'm as fit as a Mallee bull. You know, it's crazy, but I don't for the life of me understand what made me go on those binges in the first place. I mean, the drink and the drugs.'

'Laura told me.'

'Oh. Yeah? Well, of course, you helped get me to her apartment in Manly, didn't you?'

'Yes.'

'Phew! I must have been a right mess!'

'We all were.'

'Yeah… Well, you know, self-pity being the vice and all that. I mean, a bloke can always do other, more sensible things, can't he?'

'Sure can.'

82

'Listen, will you let me thank you, for crying out loud? Will you let me do that?'

'I'm thanked.'

'Okay. Well, all right, then. I just wanted you to know… that I like you, I mean. And as far as the booze and drugs are concerned… Well, they're finished. I mean, they're *definitely* out. No more. I mean, even if I wanted to, I wouldn't… For Laura's sake, if not for mine. She… expects so much of me now.'

I said nothing.

'You know, Laura… she's… well, she's the finest human being I know. Straight down the middle, no holds barred. If it wasn't for her, I'd be six feet under by now. It's been that way all my life, as far back as I remember.'

He stopped there, fiddling with the spoon, looking around the cafe and then stirring the remains of his coffee.

'I never told you,' he said, as if he had known me for twenty years instead of a few months, 'but Laura and I came from what you might call a wealthy family. Now people who earn their money, they're usually pretty straight, but people who just *collect* money, well, they're usually a poor breed. My father inherited his money and didn't try to do anything with it but spend it. My mother married him for it. He knew it and resented her for it, but they had children anyway, though they didn't much care for us. They only had us because they were Catholic and didn't believe in contraception. It didn't mean they had to like us. The first time they really knew I was alive was when they saw that I could play the piano with more than normal skill. This appealed to their snobbery. For this reason, they encouraged me. Apart from that, there was nothing.'

He paused, fidgeting uneasily with the collar of his shirt, then went on: 'They used to fight all the time. They'd do it in front of us. The language used wasn't what you'd expect from people of their social standing. They were repeatedly unfaithful to each other and they let one another – and us – know it. So Laura and I, in a sense, had no choice. We stuck close together and had few friends. When Laura was nineteen she got engaged to a man, an architect, who our father didn't think was worthy of our good name. I don't know what he said to that man – maybe he just bought him off – but Laura never saw him again and she became pretty bitter. When I was nineteen, I smashed my fingers in that accident, so couldn't play professionally any more, and after that my parents lost interest in me. So I went downhill and something twisted in Laura, making her harder, more cynical, not caring about anyone but me. What a mess all round!'

He finally looked directly at me, his face pained. 'But Laura,' he said, 'I wish you'd known her better. Because she's clean. She's really clean.'

Silence. Around us, the other customers were chattering, the trays were clattering, the outside traffic was growling and honking, but strangely, where we sat, it seemed silent. Jim had lowered his face again and was fidgeting with his empty cup, clearly embarrassed by what he had told me.

For a moment, I was tempted to repay him with my side of the coin, but instead I got to my feet and said, 'Thanks. Now I understand a few things.' He grinned sheepishly, we shook hands and then I left.

As I was leaving, Jack Collins, grinning but silent, walked in. Our shoulders brushed and then he was gone. I stopped outside to look back into the cafe, through the large plate-glass window. Collins walked straight across the cafe and took the chair facing Jim Wentworth. I was frightened, but there was nothing I could do.

*   *   *

I lay beside her on the bed, smoking a cigarette and staring up at the ceiling. Never, after we had finished, had we lain in each other's arms. We had always turned onto our backs, as if we were strangers.

'Laura,' I said, 'I'm moving out.' I hadn't told her about my meeting with her brother.

Silence.

'Did you hear me?'

'Yes. You're going.'

'Well?'

'Well?'

'Isn't there anything you want to say? No accusations? Not even that you knew it would come to this?'

'When are you leaving?'

I turned my head to stare at her. The last, fading rays of the sun were filtering through the window, down across her face. In this dusty, golden twilight her profile was lovely, if taut. Her lips were tight; nothing was revealed. I stared up at the ceiling again.

'Tomorrow,' I said. 'Maybe the next day. No later than Saturday. What does it matter?'

'It doesn't.'

'No regrets?'

'I expected nothing.'

'That's not an answer.'

'It's all I have.'

'Then it's finished tonight.'

'Yes,' she said, 'I suppose it is.'

Naked, she slid off the bed and stood by the side of the window, looking out at the falling sun. Her body was sublime, as rigid as a statue, her face as unrevealing as the dark side of the moon. She stood like that for a long time, the silence unbroken. Then, without a word, without even glancing at me, she dressed quickly and left.

I turned my face to the wall.

*   *   *

I didn't leave the next day, nor the day after that, and on the Saturday I was continuing the walk I had started a few hours after she left the room. Something kept hammering incessantly in my head, my stomach was churning. I felt like someone chained to a treadmill: my legs kept moving but I wasn't getting anywhere.

Shortly after she left I had packed my travel bag, thrown my jacket over my shoulders and walked out of the room, leaving the packed bag behind me. I started off by doing a bar crawl around most of the Cross and awakened the next morning stretched out on a bench in Hyde Park. After that, I just walked an endless mile, following whichever direction my restless feet cared to lead me. They led me far and wide to nowhere special, but I kept walking until I felt that my legs were going to collapse under me.

Well, though physically only walking, I was actually running again, though not really running away because my packed bag was still back in that damned rooming house. I had to go back there for the bag, but I'd be damned if I'd go back, so I just kept walking, and walking, my hands in my trouser pockets, my head lowered in confusion and shame, my shoulders stooped like those of an old man. For sure I wasn't proud of myself.

By Saturday morning, I had thought so much about the whole situation, I felt that I was losing my mind. And the more I thought about it, the crazier it all seemed to be. I no longer knew if I loved or hated the bitch, if she loved or hated me. The way she had stood up, calmly, stark naked, to stand interminably beside the window, looking out at the sunset, then silently dressed herself and left, was beginning to haunt me. I recalled that taut profile caught in dusk's golden light, all emotion held in check with an iron will. And I recalled her tormented brother leaning across the cafe table, closer to me, his eyes bright for a change as he told me about the sister who was not remotely as I had imagined her. What was locked up inside her? What was she feeling? What had she seen in me, if anything? To hell with it, I'd run again. To hell with it, I wouldn't run. In truth, I didn't have a clue what I would do, so I just kept walking, endlessly walking, out of the park and back into the Cross, into the dense crowds and the chaotic traffic, back into the bars and the booze, with little hope of retreating.

But I managed to retreat. And come Saturday afternoon, I was sick, sad, bewildered and beaten. Crossing the Sydney Harbour Bridge, I looked down and saw the sail boats colourfully at play in calm blue waters. I felt like diving down there and drowning. The sun was still high in the sky, burning into my brain, and I cursed the city and the sun and the whole damned world. Then I froze where I stood.

Laura was standing in the middle of the bridge, wearing her dark-blue sweater and green slacks. Her long, raven hair had been undone and was being blown out behind her by the wind. She was leaning against the railing, smoking a cigarette and looking calm to the point of non-existence. I walked up to her, stopped silently behind her, and then, not too sure of what I meant, no longer giving a damn, I said softly, 'Laura Wentworth, I love you.'

For a while she didn't move. Then, ever so slowly, as if in a trance, she turned around and looked at me with those deep, liquid eyes. She opened her mouth to say something, but quickly closed it again. Instead of speaking, she just smiled, then shook her head from side to side, until finally, unexpectedly, she stumbled slightly as if drunk, then fell forward into my arms, clutched me tightly and wept.

'Oh, thank God!' she said. 'Thank God!'

Chapter Six

WEB OF PAIN

Leaning back against the pillows, her skin pale and smooth in the gloom, her cigarette glowing and reflected from her eyes, she said, 'I'd been waiting and waiting for it, expecting it, but when you said it I didn't want to hear it, I couldn't bring myself to believe it, and I knew that if I attempted to say too much, if I so much as moved a muscle, I'd fall apart and possibly never recover. I didn't want to hold you like that – not by your pity – and I felt, just as that sun was going down, so was my life. I love you. I didn't want to love you. But I love you and now I'm at your mercy.'

'You're safe.'

'I don't believe in safety. We always walk a tightrope and accident can throw us either way. You can't know today what you might do tomorrow, but believe me, I'm now willing to take that chance. You owe me nothing. I love you selfishly, for myself, not for your benefit. Do you understand that? It's the purest form of greed in the world.'

'Then selfish we both are.'

'You're going to run again, aren't you? Finally, you're going to run. And you always will.'

'No, not this time.'

'Well, maybe I will. Who knows? Sometimes I feel that I'm borderline hysterical. I'm up and I'm down. I don't even know if I'm capable of sustaining this relationship. All of my life it's been a fight, trying to hold on to something special, the possibility of true love, a feeling of rapture, a sense of purity that can't be defiled; but they're always there, the faceless people, the ones you see in the streets with their false smiles and empty words, they're always there to tear everything down, to trample what's good and just into the dirt. And if it isn't the other people, it's the accidental nature of life itself. Like what happened to Jim, smashing his pianist's fingers in an act of celebration he probably didn't even want in the first place. I think we live too much for others. That's why I want our affair, while and if it lasts, to be one of selfishness on both sides. I want no claims on either of us.'

'You've got a claim on me.'

'No, I haven't. I'm here by consent. You owe me nothing. I wouldn't be here under any other terms.'

'You mean I can leave when I wish?'

'Yes, that's what I mean.'

'Yet you say you love me.'

'That's why I put no claims upon you. What's the point of loving under false pretences?'

'What's the point in enduring pain?'

'You can't avoid pain by pretending it isn't there.'

'No, I tried that. I walked the streets for days, trying that, but it didn't work. So I want you to know, just for the record, and before I possibly run away again, that I've never felt the kind of pain I felt over you, except maybe the pain I felt over my father.'

'Why did you run from him?'

'Because, in failing myself, I failed him. Because his last words to me were a condemnation that I couldn't refute. Let's face it, complete honesty is something that few of us possess. We may think we have it, but it slips away from us and we rationalise – God, how we rationalise! – all the lies we tell to ourselves. In truth, I believe my failures helped kill my father.'

'It happens.'

'It doesn't have to.

'No, it doesn't have to. But we seem to spend our lives doing damage to each other, by default, with the best of intentions. We're emotional cannibals, devouring each other and then mourning the departed.'

'That sounds harsh.'

'But it's true. Don't you see? We're told to live for the benefit of others, but it's not really possible to do that without causing damage. I desperately try to live for my weak brother while he, despite his weaknesses, is desperately trying to live for me. Each encourages the other to become dependent and then we both fall flat on our faces, wondering what happened. Is it right?'

'I hadn't thought of it that way.'

'Well, think about it. I hadn't thought about Jack Collins, about what drives him to do what he does. But think: he's a half-cast Abo, white dad, black mum, both alcoholic, bringing up their only child, Collins, out there in the sticks of Queensland. Despite this, their child, Collins, has a brain as sharp as a razor. Wasted. So he lights out of there when still just a teenager. And ends up in Kings Cross, with the junkies and the drunkards and the whores. We've backed him and his kind into a corner where life means nothing but constant struggle – against racist insults, enforced charity, victimisation. We've forced him into a corner where the only way he can survive with dignity is to close all his windows, barricade his doors, refuse all potentially threatening relationships, particularly with white people, and lash out before anyone gets too close.'

'There was a thing about him I couldn't quite grasp. I actually liked him. Even after what he did to Jim, I couldn't help but secretly admire him. Now I see why.'

'I'll tell you something. When Jim started come out of his long illness, the drink and the drugs, when he started talking again, we got into a conversation about Collins. When Jim said that he admired Collins because Collins never asked for favours and never gave any, I cut Collins down with every foul word my tongue could utter. Jim wasn't shocked by my profanity, but he gave me the most forceful look I've ever seen in him, and he said, "Don't despise Collins for trying to destroy me. The man loves me in his own way – and that's something he simply can't afford.' Then he added something that frightened me even more: "If I thought that my ruination would help Collins, I'd help him find that salvation. I owe him that much."'

For a moment, she lay there quietly, scarcely breathing, looking up at the ceiling. Then she said: 'It's all so strange and foolish. I came to these conclusions when I was standing on the Sydney Harbour Bridge, looking out over the city, imagining it as a great web trapping us all. And then, when I heard you speak and turned around to face you, I knew that nothing would matter anymore, except you and me and our selfish, greedy, precarious love; and that I no longer cared if Jim found out about us, that I would tell him myself and not worry about the consequences. And yet I brought you here, to my own apartment, because I didn't want him to find us together… and because I knew he wouldn't be here.'

The blood rushed to my face – and then suddenly I turned cold, very cold.

'Where is he now?' I asked.

'That's why I'm frightened,' she said. 'You see, three days ago, when I left you in the rooming house and returned to this place, he was gone. I haven't seen him since.'

*   *   *

It was like a blow to the pit of my stomach. I closed my eyes, pressed the back of my head into the pillow, and thought, What now? What now? Stars were spinning in the darkness behind my eyelids, a veritable cosmos, and out of it sprang all the memories I would rather have shed.

I thought of this girl, this woman, and of the unspeakable agonies she must have been going through in the three days preceding her walk to that bridge. I thought of the cigarettes she would have smoked and the coffee she would have drank and the walls she would have stared at as the hours ticked by, slower and slower, through the anguished days and harrowing, silent nights. I thought of the love she had for me and of the pain of loss she must have borne and of how it must have mingled with the mystery of her brother into the voiceless screaming of stripped nerves.

'Oh, no!' I whispered, though thankfully she didn't hear me.

Behind my closed eyelids, Jack Collins was staring at me, his gaze hard and bright, as he said, *I love that boy and this is a weakness, so I must kill it.* And he added: *If I accelerate his pain into his destruction, will you prevent it*?

'Into thin air,' Laura was saying. 'Just like a puff of smoke. Oh, God, I'm scared!'

Then the dark street was there and Collins' victim was backing away, pleading, *No, please, I…* and Collins, finally driven beyond the brink to which society had sent him, was moving in to cut down the

93

generalised enemy, the white fella, with his knife. And then we were both running away from the scene of the crime, straight back to the rooming house, where Collins again stared at me, his eyes at once mocking and tormented, from across a blue-smoke room. *I will not forget this.*

'Where could he *be*?' Laura asked, talking to herself rather than to me. 'All this *time!*'

What was it, exactly, that Collins would not forget? And how would he pay us back for whatever it was? A chill of fear shot through me at the thought of this, because at that very moment I recalled how, just as I was leaving the cafe, Collins had entered to sit down with Jim. And Jim had not been seen since then.

No, Collins had said, *I want you to stay.*

'I think he's back with Collins,' I said to Laura.

'Oh, no!'

'I saw him. Just before I sent you away from the rooming house. It was in a cafe near the El Alamein Fountain. We didn't talk about much... general things... but Jim *did* seem pretty uneasy. Then, when I was leaving, I saw Collins entering the cafe and joining Jim at the table. That made *me* feel uneasy.'

'And you haven't been back to the rooming house since? You've just been walking the streets?'

'Yes.'

She turned around and rolled into my arms, her face pressed to my chest. The warmth was diminished by the fear in which we now held each other.

'Hold me!' she said. 'Hold me!'

'Easy. Easy.'

'He's drinking again. I *know* it. Drinking again and probably back on drugs.'

'Yes. Probably.'

'Do you think Collins will tell him?'

94

'Tell him what?'

'About us.'

'Possibly. I'm not sure.'

'I don't care. *It doesn't matter anymore*!'

'It does and you do. Be quiet.'

'We'll go and find him. We'll – '

'No.'

'Please!'

'Not now. It won't do any good.'

'I feel so helpless.'

'You can't help Jim any more. You just said it in other words: finally, he has to stand by himself. Sooner or later, he has to make his own decisions.'

'Collins will *use* him!'

'We can't stop that.'

'We can *try*!'

'It's hopeless.'

'Andy, listen, please, you've got to promise me something…'

Letting her voice trail off, she sat upright, held me by the shoulders, dug her fingers in and said fiercely, passionately, 'We have to stick together. You and me. No matter what happens, no matter what becomes of Jim and Collins, if you and me stick together we'll survive it. You understand? It's too late for me now. I no longer have the strength to go it alone. I'm breaking my vows and I'm staking my claim… Andy, I *need* you. You understand what I'm saying? It's *need*, Andy. *Need*!'

And then she broke, she wept, she pressed her whole body against mine and then we sank back down, and there it was again, the terror, and the pain coming out in wretched, choked, bitter sobbing that stripped me bare, left me defenceless, riven with a despair I could scarcely control. So I went that journey with her, borne

95

along on the tears of our grieving, her moans amplified in my ears, our breath mingling in the sulphurous heat of our rage and grief.

'Now!' she whispered, weeping against my chest. '*Now!*'

But like a nightmare, the door burst open and Collins was standing there, a harsh light in his eyes, a triumphant grin on his face, and he hurled the drunk or stoned Jim Wentworth into the room, shouting, 'Go to your sister, Jim! Go to your white angel!'

Laura screamed.

*   *   *

Looking back on it, even years later, would be like thinking back on a recurrent dream. Jim Wentworth lay sprawled across the bedroom carpet, his legs tucked under his chin like a fetus in the womb, his eyes covered by his arms, alternately moaning and mumbling some incoherent protestation against the reality of what he had just seen: his beloved sister in bed with his friend. And still standing triumphantly in the doorway, laughing viciously as Laura twisted backward to face the wall, her scream dying into choked sobbing, was the dark and dangerous Jack Collins.

I remember sliding somehow to the floor, slipping into my trousers, turning back to take everything in with a calm feeling that had surely gone beyond all reasoning. Then I went towards the door, watching in a trance as Collins backed out, still laughing, laughing, and I punched him, punched him again, punched him a third time until the blood flecked the ridge of my knuckles; but Collins' laughter continued, he did not fall over. Even as I kept hitting him, as the blood poured from his nose, there was no sign of weakness, no attempt to defend himself, just the laughter, that mockery of my violence, my black rage, my tears of self-loathing and desperation.

'Go down! Go down!' I bawled, begging him to release me, pleading with him for an escape, but the laughter continued and I had to keep hitting him, feeling the warm blood on the back of my hands, my knuckles, until it dissolved, all of it, into a deeper crimson haze. Then Laura's fingers were digging into my shoulders, pulling me off Collins, dragging me away as her tears fell with mine. And as I stumbled backward into the web of our mutual pain, I heard a final, weak burst of laughter from Collins, then he turned away and was gone, his footsteps retreating down the stairs, and then I fell to my knees at Laura's feet, panting breathlessly, finished.

'Oh, God,' I heard her say. 'What has he done to my brother?'

I closed my eyes.

*   *   *

The circle was complete. All we had gained, we had once more lost. Laura had sank to the floor to take her drunken or drugged brother into her arms, and I was left there, alone, momentarily forgotten as they rocked together in a tableau of love and hatred. I felt my own tears being held in check, stifled, as my rage against all of them mounted. I was feeling betrayed.

'I'm sorry, Jim. Please, please, forgive me.'

'Bitch!' he responded wildly. 'You whore!'

It was then that I understood fully the true meaning of selflessness, of those who devour love only to weep for its loss, and I reached across to pull Laura away from this whipped and craven thing, shook her by the shoulders and said, 'Don't let him do this to you. Don't let him chain us all. Can't you see, Laura? He's weak and he's frightened and this is his way of keeping you

97

enslaved. Laura, listen to me! He'll take your heart and your mind and he'll feed off them until there's nothing left of you, of me, of whatever is that's grown between us.'

'Bastard!' he screamed, and when I looked around I saw the twisted features of a mean, petulant child, a moral cannibal whining for the only thing that alone would help him survive: the unquestioning love and obedience of his sister.

'Get out,' I said to him, sensing myself to be close to murder. 'Get the hell out of here.'

Laura slapped my face.

'Leave him alone!' she cried. 'Can't you see what we've done to him? Do you want to complete what Collins started?'

Lowering my face, I covered my ears with my hands and whispered, 'Collins only gave Jim what he had always wanted.'

'No!' Jim exclaimed, getting slowly, unsteadily, to his feet and backing across the room. 'That's a lie.'

'You wanted someone to take responsibility for you.'

'I did not.'

'If not Laura, then Collins. You wanted to hold her by her pity for you. Because you knew that she was strong and you were weak and that you couldn't survive alone. Then, when you felt that you might be losing her, you wanted to chain her by the pain you were giving her. You looked to Jack Collins as a means to this end – and as the cross you could nail your own guilt to. It wasn't the salvation of Collins you were looking for – it was your own. At the cost of Laura's freedom and happiness.'

'No.' Now it was a whimper.

'Collins was backed into a wall, he was close to the brink. His desperation, his need to survive without feelings that could later be turned against him – those very feelings were the instruments of your plan. He was your lover, wasn't he? And you betrayed him. And now you're trying to claim your sister as well.'

'I refuse to listen to this!'

'Then get out of here.'

'Jim!' Laura screamed, reaching out to him. 'Don't go! Don't run away from it!'

But her voice was lost in the descending darkness. Sobbing, panting, mumbling incoherent protestations, Jim went out the door and was gone.

*　　　*　　　*

Laura was on her knees, leaning slightly forward, her forehead resting against the foot of the bed. One hand was covering her mouth; her eyes were wet and distant. I could barely hear her breathing. The room was dissolving into evening's darkness.

'Laura, I – '

'Don't touch me!'

'It had to happen.'

'Get out.'

'I love you.'

'Is that why you said what you said? So that Jim would lose me and you could have me?'

'No. I wouldn't want to win you that way.'

'There are no winners here. Only losers. Only need.'

'Please, Laura, don't deny what you said to me before.'

'I didn't know what I was saying. I was wrong.'

'You were right.'

'Need. Only need.'

'Is Jim's need worth your life?'

'What's my life?'

'Something worthy of love.'

'I don't need love. I need nothing.'

'Nothing but Jim's need for you?'

'Shut up!'

'Laura, listen to me. Please. If you accept this, you'll be accepting what you previously despised: that tribe of cannibals who devour each other and then mourn the departed. Will you continue to live for him, and he for you, until you both fall? And is his sickness worth it?'

'I can't let him go.'

'You have to.'

'I won't.'

'Then he'll take you down with him when he falls.'

'I don't care.'

'Laura, please – '

'*Don't touch me!*'

Turning away from her, I went to the bedside cabinet, took a cigarette from the packet and lit it. Laura didn't move. I stepped back around the bed, sat down on the floor beside her, inhaled, exhaled and stared at the deepening darkness. When I closed my eyes, I saw a ball of white light expanding and contracting repeatedly, and from it came a sharp, clear pain. I felt sick and weary and defeated, but I couldn't give in. Not this time.

'Laura, I love you. I'm not too sure what that means or what it's worth, but it's true, it's a fact. I want you, selfishly, for myself, and I won't let you go. It being that need seems to be the only criterion for the moment, I could possibly say that I need you and win you that way, but I won't; because it's your love I want, not your life; your respect, not your pity. I *want* you. I won't give you my need as a pathetic way of gaining your acceptance.'

'I would not accept you, now, under any terms.'

'Why?'

'Because you're despicable. Because you're hard and cruel and drove Jim away just to get him out of your way and out of my reach.'

'Isn't that the greatest compliment I could pay you? Could I possibly love you more?'

'I won't accept your love at the price of my brother's life.'

'Yet he'll sacrifice your life for his own.'

'That's a lie.'

'We both know it's the truth. Your brother can neither stand for, nor by, himself. He's a man whose veins can only be filled with the blood of those who pity him.'

'Please get out of here.'

'Don't make me, Laura.'

'I don't want to ever see you again.'

'Okay. But before I go, remember this. When Jack Collins called me a running man, I denied it. But he was right. All my life I've been running – from obstacles, from responsibilities, from commitments, from reality – but this time I'm not going to run. The one thing I've learnt from this sorry shambles is that you can't avoid the truth by turning your back on it and that the truth can't hurt if it's faced with clear eyes. So, I'm not running this time. If I walk out that door, it's because you sent me away. If you do, I'll expect you to shoulder the responsibility for it. Don't call it desertion and make your martyr's cross out of it.'

'I release you from all guilt.'

'Then you still want me to go?'

'Now. This minute. Please.'

I stood up, finished dressing, started leaving, but turned back in the doorway.

'What are you going to do now?' I asked.

'I'm going to rescue my brother.'

'Then you're going to imprison yourself.'

'Fuck off. Goodbye.'

I turned away and walked out.

*   *   *

Darkness had fallen. The lights of Manly had come on. I walked down to the beach where I wandered aimlessly up and down, just listening to the sea, then took a cab back to the city centre. Once there, I started walking aimlessly again, reluctant to go back to the rooming house in King's Cross, dreading what I might find there. So I shouldered my way through the crowds, feeling slightly demented, watching the electric eyes of the cars boring through the night. There was a cold wind, the clouds were low, rain was in the air. I stopped at a set of traffic lights, was hemmed in by other pedestrians, then carried relentlessly forward with the others as the green turned to red. In brightly illuminated store windows, plastic ladies stared out with vacant eyes and television sets, all turned on at the same time, displayed different programmes. On busy street corners, men selling newspapers bellowed the headlines: the latest body counts in Vietnam, a serial killer operating in the suburbs, teenagers running amok after a rock concert. Drunks all over the place, being harassed by the cops, druggies doing their deals in the shadows, the better off gorging themselves in busy restaurants, the pubs going great guns. Just another evening in the city.

Walking the teeming streets, under clouds threatening rain, I thought of how I had come to this place and of how I was getting ready to leave again. For once I wasn't leaving of my own volition and I didn't really want to go – not this time. Out of a welter of confused recollections, I recalled the triumphant laughter of Jack Collins as his head jerked back and forth, to and fro, from the impact of my knuckles. This recollection receded and was replaced by that ball of white light expanding and contracting in my head, spreading the pain. Blinking my eyes, shaking my head from side to side to clear it, I looked up to see that I was barging my way through another crowd of oncoming pedestrians.

'Hey, mind where you're going, cobber! You don't own the whole bloody street!'

There was an ambulance parked by the side of the road with its blue light flashing like a kid's toy over the faces of the spectators, over the white-jacketed male nurses, over the police, over the red sports car that was wrapped around a concrete post, its bonnet badly mangled, the young driver jammed into his seat, between twisted metal, torn upholstery and the bloody, shattered remains of what had been his left arm. Men in overalls, the wrecking crew, were all over the car, their faces ghostly in that flickering blue light, trying with crowbars to work the twisted metal away from the trapped body of the driver. The cops were trying to keep the spectators back, away from the wreckage, but the people kept pressing forward with their eyes wide, their tongues excitedly wagging when not chomping on hamburgers or licking multi-coloured ice cream cones. There was the sound of harsh weeping, coming from a bedraggled young woman who was leaning weakly forward between two cops, trying to stifle her tears with a handkerchief. The blood on her blouse indicated that she had been the passenger. More blood had splashed out of the car and was still dripping onto the road.

Pointing at the blood, a middle-aged man with a self-righteous face said, 'Serves them right for speeding. These drivers nowadays don't give a damn for man or beast!' Then a woman screamed out that the driver had just died, he was dead, and the cops kept pushing the spectators back and I quickly walked on.

The complexity of human relationships was beginning to elude me. I no longer knew what was right, what was wrong, what was the reality, what was the fantasy. I had only been here a few days, no, a few weeks – who could tell? – and already the pressure was bearing down on me like the combined weight of every high-rise in the city. Violence and death, love and hatred: what difference if life ended in a dark street or in the bloody, smashed remains of a red sports car? Did romantic love exist? And if it did, how long could it be expected to last in an unpredictable world? Blood on the road and people eating hamburgers; it didn't make sense, yet it couldn't be denied. Yes, I truly loved Laura and the aching need was still there, so this time I didn't think I could run from it.

A little old lady tried to hand me a religious pamphlet, but was interrupted by two drunks who fell arm in arm between us. One of them vomited on the pavement at her feet. After babbling their apologies, they demanded a couple of pamphlets, one for each of them, but the little old lady didn't give them to *anybody*, so with an upturned nose she hurried away to find some more acceptable sinners. Thus foiled, the drunks took to attacking each other with their fists, but soon fell backwards over a rubbish bin and lay giggling in spilt drink and wet refuse. Looking away, I saw just across the road the helmeted lamps casting their wan yellow glow over the dark greenery of the park slopes, which rose like great breasts to the night sky. In front of the park, people were queuing for buses or frantically waving down passing cabs. The road itself, filled with traffic, was a potential death trap, but I ran without looking and made it safely across.

Whether I liked it or not, I had to return to that rooming house for my travel bag and typewriter. The thought of meeting the hard, mocking stare of Jack Collins was unnerving, particularly after the way I'd beaten him up. The thought of further involvement with Jim Wentworth was repulsive. Yet there was no way out of it, unless I started running again, leaving without collecting my gear. I wasn't, this time, willing to do that, so I began cutting across the park, heading for the Cross, my feet taking me past petting lovers and drunks and people out walking their dogs. Far away, above another low hill, a few stars were managing to glitter between the rain clouds. And somewhere up there, I remembered, Laura was about to invite her own ruination.

I stopped to light another cigarette, thought of cancer on the lungs, silently said to hell with it, and walked on to William Street. Ribbons of electric lights ran uphill through the darkness to the final gaudy cavalcade at the top. The rain had started falling and I saw it glistening on the pavements between the feet of the early-evening revellers. For the first time I began feeling the tension present everywhere in the Cross and I certainly now felt it in myself. I wondered where Laura was right now, if she had found her pitiful brother, and, if so, what she was saying to him and he to her. With the possibilities chilling me, I quickened my pace.

'Could you spare us a ciggy, mate? Bless ya.'

The stench of stale beer and unwashed clothing, black stubble under a pair of bloodshot eyes. I gave him the whole damned packet and kept walking. Walking and stopping and thinking and then walking again, passing brightly-lit shops, cafes and pubs, resisting the urge to go into one of the latter. Every nerve in my belly was jumping. When a whore stepped unexpectedly out of a dark doorway, I nearly collapsed on the spot. Now I was really frightened. I was scared of what Collins would do if Laura went to that rooming house and tried to drag Jim out. Not only that: I was frightened of what Jim would do when he heard the sound of her voice. And so I walked even faster.

The rain was falling hard, jabbing viciously at the pavements, drumming brutally on the plate-glass windows, a harsh, relentless deluge that stung my face and made me close my eyes. Already, it was boiling along the gutters, taking dead matches, cigarette butts and discarded newspapers with it. Cars and buses battled every which way, sending curved, hissing fountains of water up after them. Umbrellas clashed, people were running for cover, and one young man raised his face to the downpour, spread wide his arms, and accepted it all with a cry of delight. Before I turned the corner into Darlinghurst Road, I saw a couple of cops moving in on him.

This was the centre of the Cross and now the neon lights were everywhere, winking, dancing, flickering in a crazy, kaleidoscopic fantasy. I smelt barbecued chicken, grilled hamburger and Indian curry in the air, mingled with booze and soaked vegetables. The streets were vibrant, the whole place a riot of colour and sound. I felt sick, dizzy and almost unreal, and when I tried to focus on something tangible, something concrete, the first person I saw was Mr. Fields, the demented hunchback from the rooming house. There was something I wanted to ask him, but I wasn't sure

106

what it was. I didn't have time to think of it because stooped under the heavy mound of his back, he came scurrying towards me with one walking stick swinging wildly and the other fixed firmly on the ground. This grotesque creature came out of a chaos of heavy rain and traffic, his mouth wide open, shouting words of abuse, making me instinctively back off, my arm covering my face, trying to avoid the swinging stick, a gargled sound of protest in my throat.

'Swine! Bastard! Cunt!' Fields screamed, beating me insanely about the arms and heads with his stick, backing me into the nearest wall. 'What do you care? What does *anyone* care about this pitiful excuse for a man?'

That stick kept flailing me and such was my panic that I didn't quite know what to do. It was all too fantastic, too nightmarish to be credible, and so I kept backing off, bawling, 'Stop it! Stop it!' But taking no notice, he continued attacking me, cursing me out, an inane string of obscenities, his malformed body rocking to and fro, his hunchback and twisted legs making me think of a monstrous spider on the rampage.

'Swine, bastard, cunt, what do you care?'

My back was to the wall, the blows were coming thick and fast, but even in my bewilderment I had a fleeting vision of Jack Collins' head as it jerked backward under my punching fists. And then I remembered that this crazed creature was drunk and that I was being attacked, so I stepped forward to stop him. Too late. Other hands were already grabbing him, dragging him away, and the man holding him apologised and informed me that Fields was always like this, every night, after a drop of the hard stuff.

'I'll just put him to bed,' the man said.

Still, I was badly shaken. The rain was abating, the wind was dying down, and I could feel the sweat starting on my forehead. I was trembling. I felt sick. The feeling of nightmare hadn't yet left me. My mind was still trapped in some deep, dark, twilight zone, the shadows of things that could not be defined flitting before my dazed eyes. Looking backward and down, I saw the nocturnal city as an immense web of dazzling lights and pain, the lights a shield for the pain locked within. Then I thought of an Aboriginal trapped by the colour of his skin, a girl trapped by the contradictions of her own reasoning, a brother trapped by his own weaknesses, but slyly waiting to destroy all the others. With this in mind, I hurried on my way and eventually arrived at the rooming house.

Something was wrong.

*   *   *

The whore who had greeted me during my first morning in the rooming house was there to greet me now. She was walking in a shaky manner down the few steps that led up into the building. One hand was using the iron railing for support, the other was covering her open mouth, as if to prevent her from throwing up. She was weeping, not in sadness, but in shock.

'Up there,' she said, pointing back over her shoulder in the direction of the front door. 'Up there.'

'*Laura!*'

The name came screaming out of me even before I realised what I was doing. Bounding past the weeping whore, I ran into the gloomy interior of the rooming house. I could hardly see, but I blundered my way along the downstairs hallway and turned onto the first flight of stairs.

Sheer horror had seized my thoughts. All reason had disappeared into a whirling void of nausea and fear.

'*Laura*!' I screamed again while blindly going up the stairs, cursing myself and loathing the silence that fell about me. I heard nothing. Saw nothing. Just the silence and the deepening darkness as I neared the first floor. I was bounding up the remaining stairs, taking two at a time, my hand slippery with sweat on the bannister, my heart racing, my mind almost in delirium, when, just before the last stair, I froze where I was.

Laura was on her knees, crouched over like a praying Madonna, her face covered with her hands. She was rocking lightly, neurotically, back and forth, shaking with the violence of her emotions. A beam of light shone out of her brother's room, motes of dust at play in the air. A shivering shadow fell across Laura's bowed head.

Hanging from a rope tied to a rafter was the body of Jim Wentworth, his two feet swaying above a chair that lay on its side on the floor.

Laura made no sound.

Chapter Seven

DEATH IN THE STREETS

'Don't cut him down, boys, until the photographers arrive.'

The police inspector ducked under the swaying feet and looked speculatively up and down the corridor. He was wearing a gaberdine, which seemed appropriate, and a trilby hat. His face was ruddy and pleasant. He circled warily around Jim's hanging body and then came back to me. I was leaning against the wall, still in shock, I'm sure, smoking a cigarette. None of this seemed remotely real.

'You say this is your room, kid?' he asked.

I turned my head to look sideways into my room. The light was still on. Laura was sitting on the side of my bed, hands folded primly on her lap, face blank with shock. She wasn't crying. A uniformed policeman stood nearby, looking slightly embarrassed.

'Yes,' I said, 'that's the room.'

'How long have you been here?'

'A few weeks.'

'Work?'

'Unemployed.'

'Where do you come from?'

'Perth.'

'You have a Pommie accent.'

'My parents were English immigrants. I came with them to Oz when I was four years old.'

'So you're unemployed. How do you live?'

'I have money. My father gave it to me just before he died. The bank book's originated in Perth. You can check.'

'I *know* what I can do, kid. Now let's go over it again. You say you came back here about an hour ago and found this girl kneeling on the floor, under her brother's hanging body.'

'Yes.'

'And you knew both of them?'

'Yes.'

'Where were you when the deceased hung himself?'

'Walking.'

'*All* day?'

'No.'

'Where were you about two hours ago?'

'What's the relevance of two hours?'

'It's the estimated time of death. So where were you about two hours ago?'

'Around.'

'Specifically.'

'In Manly.'

'Alone?'

'With a friend.'

'What friend?'

'Do I have to answer that?'

'We're not playing ping-pong, kid.'

'I was with… the girl.'

'This girl?'

I nodded.

'I see.' He turned his florid, pleasant face and looked at Laura. She hadn't moved from where she was sitting. The uniformed cop nearby was discreetly examining the room. 'I see,' the police inspector repeated, then started moving towards her. I touched him lightly on the arm.

'Please,' I said, 'not now. Give her a go.'

'This might be special to you, kid, but it isn't to me. I have a lot of other cases on my hands and no time to waste.' He stepped into the doorway, placed one hand on the wall, looked down at Laura and said, 'Listen, Miss, I know this might not seem like the right time, the decent time, but would you mind confirming what this fella just said?'

She looked up at him, her eyes blinking rapidly.

'Pardon?'

'Were you with him in Manly about two hours ago?'

She stopped blinking. She stared unblinkingly at the detective, then at me. After thinking about it, she said, 'Yes.' Then she dropped her gaze to the floor.

'Where?' the police inspector asked.

'In her flat,' I said.

'I was talking to the lady, kid. Where, Miss?'

'In my flat.'

'Your flat in Manly?'

'Yes.'

'And you shared that flat with your brother?'

'Yes. Recently.'

'Where was he before that?'

'Here.'

'In this room?'

'In a different room. Further along the corridor.'

'So he moved out of this place and into your flat in Manly, but then he came back here to... sorry to say this... to kill himself?'

'Yes.'

'Why did he pick Mr. White's room for his suicide?'

'Because it has an exposed rafter, I should imagine. He hung himself from the rafter. The other rooms don't have exposed rafters.'

'I'm sorry, Miss, but these questions can't be avoided.'

'It's okay. I understand.'

'So your brother wasn't in your flat in Manly when you and Mr. White were there together?'

'No, he wasn't.'

'Did you know at the time where he was?'

'No. He'd been missing for three days. That's all I knew and was concerned about.'

'I see. Listen, Miss, I don't like to have to ask you this question, but I'm afraid it can't be avoided. Just what, exactly, is your relationship with this fella?'

And he nodded to indicate me.

'We were lovers.'

'*Were*?'

'Are.'

'You work for a living, Miss?'

'Now, *wait* a minute – ' I began.

'I work,' Laura said. 'I'm an administrator for an art gallery. The Alfred Richter Gallery. In Sydney.'

'Your brother. He knew you were involved with this fella?'

Again, he nodded to indicate me.

'No.'

'He came into her flat,' I said, 'about three hours ago. He found us in bed together, then he ran out. He was really drunk, almost delirious. He was shocked when he found us.'

'Sounds like a queer one. What else?'

I shrugged. 'After he'd gone, we stayed on in the flat for about an hour. We had an argument over what

113

had happened – him finding us in bed. They – she and her brother – they were very close.'

'Go on.'

'Well, as I said, we had an argument about him. You know the kind.'

'I know.'

'I left about an hour later. She said she was going to find her brother. I caught a bus back to Sydney, walked the streets for a bit, then made my way to Kings Cross and came back here. I found her like I told you: kneeling on the landing, under his hanging body. The other woman – the one who lives in the room downstairs – she found them before I did.'

'Yes, she told us. So who else lives here?'

'Jack Collins, the owner of this place. He's an Aboriginal.'

'Must be a cute one, to own this place. What does he do?'

'Well, he owns the place. He's the landlord. I don't know anything else about him.'

'Anyone else?'

'The woman down below.'

'We *know* what she does.'

'There's also a Mr. Fields. A hunchback. He sells children's toys to passers-by in the streets. And a student painter. Name of Williams. I've only met him once and know nothing about him.'

'The other rooms?'

'Empty.'

'Were any of these people here when you arrived?'

'No. I saw Fields earlier, just a few minutes before I got here. He was at the corner of William Street and Darlinghurst Road. He was crazy drunk, but with a reasonably sober friend. The friend was going to bring him back here and put him to bed, but clearly they're not here yet.'

'Probably side-tracked into another boozer.'

'Yes. The student painter, Williams, never comes in until much later in the evening.'

'So what about Jack Collins, this Abo bright spark?'

'I don't know where he is.'

'He doesn't have a regular job?'

'No. I think he lives off the income from the rent.'

At that moment, two photographers came up the stairs, both dressed in civilian clothing, carrying cameras and flash guns. They stopped on the landing and stared up at the dangling corpse of Jim Wentworth. Jim's face was badly swollen; he was barely recognisable.

'Routine,' said one of the photographers.

'Hi, Bill,' the other photographer said to the police inspector.

'You can stay,' the police inspector said. 'The newspaper photographer can clear off. It's just a suicide, cut and dried. Nothing dramatic. So out you go, mister.'

Behind the newspaper photographer was a reporter, slim, neatly suited, red-haired, notebook and pen in hand.

'Nothing sinister at all, Inspector?'

'Nothing.'

'Motive?'

'Just mental. The usual.'

'What about a few facts?'

'See me at the station – later.'

'You caught any maniac killers recently, Inspector?'

'Get your arse out of here.'

'Let's get a coffee, mate,' the reporter said to his photographer. 'See you at the station, Inspector.'

'Sure.'

The reporter left with his friend and the remaining photographer went to work. Jim's body was no longer swaying eerily, but the photographer still moved carefully around the corpse, checking for the best angles, turning on his flash gun. 'Who's the girl?' he asked.

'Sister.'

'You want a shot of her?'

'Just for the record.'

'Looks like a nice lady.'

'Yep.'

The photographer placed himself in the doorway and focused on Laura. She didn't look up and he didn't ask her to. When the flashgun went off, she didn't budge. The photographer stepped back and asked the police inspector if he'd found anything more about the recent knife killing here in the Cross. The police inspector sighed.

'No,' he said. 'Not a thing. Just another late-night brawl that ended badly. Has the ambulance arrived yet?'

'It's at the front door. Ready, willing and able.'

'Many spectators?'

'The usual. Neighbours and passers-by.'

'Okay. Send the medics up with the stretcher when you leave. And let me have those photos just as soon as you can.'

'She's uncle.'

The photographer left and the ambulance team came up the stairs, bringing the stretcher and a covering sheet. Jim's shadow stretched across the floor. One of the medics looked at the overturned chair and asked, 'What about this?'

'You can use it.'

The medic set the chair upright, just under the dangling corpse, then he stood on the chair, stared curiously at Jim's swollen face and said, 'This one's still warm.' He started untying the rope. The other medic stood beneath him, holding on to Jim's legs, one hand up to grasp at the back of Jim's trouser belt. The rope came free and fell to the floor. The medic standing on the chair cradled Jim's head in his arms, then, slowly, both medics lowered the body on to the stretcher.

'You watch the telly last night?'

'Steptoe?'

'Yeah.'

'Hilarious. Hell, this one's as light as a feather.'

They draped the white sheet over Jim's face and body, tied it down with straps attached to the two sides of the stretcher, then picked the stretcher up between them and started down the stairs. One of them nearly tripped, cursed, grabbed the bannister with one hand to steady himself, then continued on down. He and his mate, still carrying the stretcher between them, disappeared through the front door.

'Tell me, Miss, what made your brother hang himself?'

The police inspector's question was unexpected, direct and brutal. Laura responded by staring at him with wide, dazed eyes.

'Pardon?'

'What made him put his head in a noose?'

Laura closed her eyes.

'I don't know.'

'What about you, kid?'

'Does anyone ever know?'

'That's not smart, kid.'

'I'm really not sure. He was an alcoholic...' I decided not to mention the drugs... 'He was always... well, hypersensitive. He'd been going down the drain, and then, when he found me with his sister in her apartment – '

'In bed?'

He was looking right at me.

'Yes,' I said, 'in bed. When he found us, he sort of fell to pieces. He ran out. He probably came straight here. And he killed himself. But who, finally, knows why?'

'He must have thought a lot of his sister.'

'Yes.'

'Sounds like a typical Kings Cross clown.'

'I wouldn't know.'

'Maybe not.'

He took out a packet of cigarettes and offered me one. I accepted. Then he turned to Laura and asked her if she wanted one.

'No... No, thanks.'

'Miss, I'm afraid I'm going to have to take you down to the station for further questioning. We need a full and proper record. Names, addresses, parents, where you work, ages... that sort of thing. I'd like to spare you this, but it can't be avoided. Anyway, the sooner it's over, the better. Think you can make it?'

'Yes.'

'Good. Let's go. You, too,' he added, nodding at me.

Laura stood up, swayed a little from side to side with one hand up to her forehead, was steadied by the hand of the uniformed cop. She walked out of the room, onto the landing, and glanced at me with a stricken, bewildered look on her face. For a moment, I thought she was going to reach out and touch me, but she didn't. Instead, she looked up to where her brother's body had been hanging, then looked at the floor where the stretcher had lain. She closed her eyes; a brief spasm shook her. Then she went down the stairs.

We all followed her down.

*   *   *

The rain had stopped falling. Dark clouds still hung low over the chilly night. The wan glow of the street lights fell over wet, glistening pavements and the faces of the whispering spectators. Those curious faces formed a pale, curved fence around us. The policemen kept pushing them back as they tried to inch forward. I recalled the red sports car twisted around the concrete post, other spectators looking on in fascination. The allure of a death that isn't your own.

Two squad cars were parked at the kerb. The whore from downstairs, her face streaked with dried tears, was being shown into the second car. The uniformed policeman was holding the door of the first car open. Laura looked back blankly at the rooming house, then she stooped over and clambered into the squad car. The police inspector was looking with disdain at the surrounding spectators.

'It's a circus,' he said. 'It always is.'

He motioned for me to get into the rear of the squad car, beside Laura. I stooped down to get in and then, with my hands on either side of the door-frame, I stopped. Laura had raised her head and was staring steadily at me. Once more I realised just how lovely she was. For the first time since I had come across her on that landing, there was recognition in her eyes – and no antagonism.

'It's finished,' I said.

'Yes,' she responded, 'it's finished.'

I sat beside her and looked out the front window of the car. The street receded into a darkness erratically illuminated by the street lights. The spectators were reluctantly dispersing, forced away by the cops. The cops were experienced and weary and unpopular. There was an unusual, heavy silence over all. The noise of the Kings Cross traffic seemed to be very distant. Reaching out, I took her hand in my own.

'From here on in,' she said, her voice soft but no longer remote, 'let's not beg for the salt to be rubbed into the wounds.'

I nodded in appreciation of this.

'Hey, you!'

I looked around. The police inspector was standing with one foot in the squad car, his body leaning out, one hand on the roof. His other arm was raised, index finger pointing at a dark figure that was making its way up the steps, about to enter the rooming house. The dark figure turned around to look at the police inspector, who had called out to him. I recognised Jack Collins.

'For God's sake, Jack,' I whispered, not quite knowing if I spoke for him or myself, 'don't say anything.'

But I spoke too late.

Collins stood tensely on the steps, half of him in shadow. The police inspector moved back out of the squad car and started walking toward Collins. When he reached the lower steps, he stopped. I saw him speak to Collins and Collins talking back. Then the police inspector nodded towards our squad car and began to turn around, one hand slightly raised as if to bring Collins with him.

'Look out!' a policeman shouted, and then Collins had lifted his left leg and kicked out with his booted foot. The kick took the police inspector on his right shoulder, sending him spinning off the steps to sprawl spreadeagled on the pavement. He went into a fast, neat roll and was on his feet again just as Collins shouted something incoherent and virtually dived through the doorway, into the rooming house, slamming the heavy door behind him.

'Collins – no!' I shouted and was leaping from the squad car just as the police inspector was hurrying back up the steps to tug on the closed, and clearly locked, front door. A pair of hands grabbed me and roughly pushed me back against the side of the squad car. 'Don't make a move, mate,' said a deep voice as the hands shook me gently, insistently. Looking over the man's shoulder, I saw a uniformed cop racing along the pavement to join his boss, the police inspector, on the steps.

There was the sound of smashing glass. A chair flew out of the lower front window and I saw the snout of a pistol, spitting a brief flash of fire. The sound of the shot ricocheted along the street and the uniformed cop, grabbing instinctively at his side, went spinning around and collapsed to the pavement. A woman screamed and the remaining spectators scattered. Then Collins' voice came ringing out of the broken window.

'Yes!' he shouted. 'I stabbed your precious white fella! Now come and get me, you bastards!'

I hid my face in the cold steel of the squad car.

*　　　*　　　*

Collins didn't shoot again. Two policemen ran around the squad cars and started dragging their fallen comrade away. The man was moaning piteously and shaking his head from side to side, dazed and disbelieving. The

121

police inspector backed down the steps, his eyes fixed on that shattered window. 'Come on out, fella!' he shouted as he backed towards the first squad car. 'There's no way out the back of that building, so you're trapped in there.'

'You keep going backward, copper. Because the minute you take a step forward, I'll have your guts for garters.'

'You're being foolish.'

'More foolish to come out.'

The police inspector came back to our squad car and reached inside for the phone. After contacting headquarters, he relayed the situation, then said, 'I want another ambulance up here ASAP and I want another squad car. We might have to cordon off the street. Bring some gas grenades. I think this one may refuse to come out.' Turning to the driver, he said, 'Turn this car around and drive to the top of the street. Park sideways across the road and let no spectators through. Understood? Good.' He looked down at Laura. 'Well, Missy,' he said with a sheepish grin, 'looks like we just might have to earn our money today.'

'Don't... Try not to... hurt him.'

'We always try, Miss; we don't always succeed. Get back in the car, Mr. White.'

I slipped into the rear seat and took hold of one of Laura's hands. The driver reversed, turned the car around and headed up to the top of the street where he parked sideways across the road, as ordered. He then got out of the car and wandered to and fro, keeping back the curious onlookers. I turned to face Laura. She was looking straight ahead, her face lined with weariness and shock.

'That night at the party,' she said. 'That was the night after the... killing.'

'Yes.'

'And the day before… that was when I first met you. You were with Collins. You… left together,'

'Yes.'

'Did you know about the… killing?'

'I was with him at the time.'

'Oh.'

'I didn't have anything to do with it. In one sense, Collins couldn't avoid it. We came out of a club, there were a few men behind us, all drunk, and they started to goad him about being an Abo, as if he was some kind of brainless ape. They wanted to play football with his black head.'

'Oh.'

'Yes. Well, one of them had a bottle. He smashed the bottle to use it as a weapon. Collins took out a flick-knife – and there they were. After that, it was more or less inevitable. There was a tussle, Collins moved in, the other man fell. He was dead. And we ran.'

'Then he decided to have a party.'

'Yes. The killing shook him up, though he tried not to show it. He had to convince himself that it didn't matter. But I think the party was a self-inflicted torture. He had to put himself through hell and endure it without flinching. That's one of the reasons Jim ended up on top of that table, degrading himself. Collins didn't respect Jim's weakness, but in his own, strange way he loved Jim. Because Jim was the only white person who'd ever treated him as an equal human being.'

'Jim was his lover, for fuck's sake.'

'His voluntary lover. Jim knew that Collins couldn't afford to let stand anything that he admired or loved too much, so Jim deliberately worked to gain Collins' affection. He did this knowing full well that

Collins would try to destroy him for it – and he wanted someone to shoulder the guilt for his own inability to face life. I know it sounds crazy, I know it's complex, but Jim was so dead inside he had to feel that he was in someone else's hands – that was Collins – and he had to feel that there was someone in his own hands – that was you. It was sacrifice all around, with Jim planted in the centre – the masochist. And like all men bent on self-destruction, Jim had to take everyone else down with him. It's complex, it's devious, it's insane – but along that street, Jack Collins is trapped by it.

'Talk to him.'

*　　*　　*

The police driver let me go. I walked back along the street with sickness in my belly and a certain amount of fear in my heart. I wasn't sure that Collins would listen to me – and I couldn't be sure that he wouldn't take a shot at me. But I had to try; for once in my badly failed life I had to give it a go. I recalled Collins' statement: 'I could almost swear that you and Jim Wentworth are one and the same.' Well, he hadn't been too far wrong, so now was the time to put things right.

The second ambulance and the extra squad car had arrived from the other end of the street. By the time I got there, they had the wounded policeman on the stretcher and were lifting him up into the ambulance. He was moaning and sobbing simultaneously. I could see his legs twitching. There was a lot of blood on the pavement where he had been lying.

No more shots had been fired and the police were spread out across the street, waiting for further instructions. The parked squad cars had their ceiling lights rotating, blue and red, blue and red, falling erratically over the taut faces of the men. The police inspector was standing beside his parked car, a megaphone in his hand. He had been talking through it to Collins for quite some time, but looked like he was about to give up. 'If you don't come, fella,' he now said, 'we'll have to gas you out.'

'You want me out there, copper, you'll have to drag me out in chains. I'm not about to volunteer for crucifixion.'

One of the policemen stopped me when I came close to the squad car.

'I want to speak to the inspector,' I said.

The inspector heard me and turned around. 'Let him through,' he said.

The policeman lowered his hand and I walked on. The inspector placed the megaphone on the bonnet of his car, ruefully rubbed his lips and said, 'Well, Mr. White, your Jack Collins is quite a lad.'

'Let me talk to him. He might listen.'

'Why?'

'Pardon?'

'Why would he listen to you?'

'I think he might have a certain amount of... regard for me.'

'Didn't know you were that close.'

'I was with him when he stabbed that man a few days back.'

The ambulance roared into life, pulled away from the kerb, started off along the street. The inspector stood there, rubbing his lips and watching as it disappeared around the distant corner. Then he looked at the rooming house and back to me.

'I see,' he said.

'It wasn't murder. They came at him, three of them. They came at him with a broken bottle and he – '

'Later, Mr. White. The night, it would appear, is still young. You willing to repeat that statement later?'

'Yes.'

'And you believe you can talk him out of there?'

'I can try.'

He handed me the megaphone.

'No,' I said, not taking it. 'I'll go over there and talk to him. Through the broken window.'

'He might not be in the mood, friend or no friend.'

'I'll chance it.'

'You want a medal?'

'Up you, too.'

He grinned. 'Okay, Mr. White, be my guest. I'll get my marksmen to keep you covered. But between you and me, that doesn't mean much. That Abo knows how to fire that pistol and you'll be as tempting as a Melbourne Bitter.'

'Can I go now?'

'Ready, set.'

I started forward. On the outer rim of my vision I could see the blurred forms of the surrounding policemen, shadowed spectres in the fluctuating blue-red night. The wind had gathered in strength, blowing into my face, chilling the sweat on my brow. The other side of the road seemed to be very far away, the rooming house half in darkness. Laura sat in the squad car at the top of the street, thinking of me, I hoped, as I was thinking of her; that, at least, might be saved. And my father's wasted, dying face, already fading in my memory with the passing of time… could I now make amends? Never before had I heard my own footsteps with such clarity, magnified, unreal. I thought: None of this can possibly be happening. It's just a bad dream.

'That's it, Mr. White.'

I stopped. I was standing just in front of the rooming house. The steps leading up into it were only a couple of feet away with the shattered window slightly

126

to my right. Collins' face was visible at the far edge of the window frame, half hidden in shadow, one eye gleaming out of his dark skin. Then I saw the glint of his teeth and I knew he was smiling, though it wouldn't have been a welcoming smile. Now I knew what real fear was – for him and for me.

'I want to talk to you, Jack.'

'I didn't think you were here to sing.'

'Are you going to listen?'

'While you stand there with your jaws gaping, I've no choice.'

'Jack, if you come out, they'll – '

'First names at last! Ringading!'

'If you come, they'll go lightly on you. It was self-defence. I've told them that. I'll be a friendly witness for you.'

'With a white lawyer defending the murderous Abo in a white man's courtroom reeking of white-victim sympathy. No thanks, white fella.'

'It won't be like that.'

'What about the copper? The one I shot. Do you think that'll swing the odds in my favour? Even if he survives, they'll have my guts for it; if he dies, then so will I. They'll make sure of it. And, brother, did I see that wound! I damned near blew his stomach out. That's *one* character who's unlikely to live out this night. How many dead now, Mr. White? That slob a few nights back, Jim Wentworth, that copper. Quite an achievement… Only it wasn't all my doing, was it?'

'No.'

'Wentworth. Suicide with a rope. That I *hadn't* planned on. Madness, madness, madness, that's all it is. He *wanted* degradation – you know that? – he actually *wanted* it. But he needed someone to act for him. Suicide. Wow. I didn't think he would go that far. If I'd

127

known that, I wouldn't have… Yes, I would. Because we learn too late.' A lengthy pause, then: 'White, did he fool us all?'

'Yes.'

'So here I am.'

'Yes.'

He chuckled, deeply, bitterly. I heard it even from where I stood.

'Well, White,' he said, 'that, in its way, is truly admirable. Because that, sure as God, is the only time that any man ever caught me hands down. Not only that, but he played for such high odds – and he won. At the price of his life, maybe, but then he never really wanted that in the first place. He was a man for death. He worshipped death. And he cheated us all to get it. That's quite an accomplishment. White, get off that pavement before I blast you off.'

'If you don't come out voluntarily, they'll gas you out.'

'They won't gas this pistol in my hand.'

'How many of them can you shoot?'

'Enough to make them shoot back.'

'You want to die, like Wentworth?'

'No, man, not like Wentworth. I don't want to die, but they won't let me live. Do you understand that? It's gone on too long, I've come too far. Now, I can die on my feet or I can die on my knees, but I can't live. They've taken the choice from me. If I walk out this door with my hands up, it'll make little difference. They'll kill me anyway. They'll just take a little longer about it to make sure it's legal. Death in the streets I can accept. Humiliation would be equivalent to suicide. If I let them put me in prison, I'll be committing suicide even before that rope goes around my neck. White, listen to me and listen good. I've been running down a blind alley all of my life, but at least I've been running on my own two feet. There aren't too many Aboriginals can say that. It's the one thing I won't let them deny me now.'

'The police constable's dead.'

That was all. The statement had boomed out through the megaphone in an oddly indifferent tone of voice. Then there was silence. No further pronouncements. As if anything further was irrelevant. It was a condemnation, a promise, a sentence of death,, sure and unmistakable. When I looked around, I saw the inspector place the megaphone back on the bonnet of his car, then lean against the vehicle and cross his arms in a nonchalant manner. I had to turn away.

'You get the message?' Collins asked.

'Come out to me with your hands up and I'll walk you back to the police. At least we can *try*.'

'I'm not going to crawl in any white man's courtroom.'

'What does it matter if it gives you a chance?'

'There's no lawyer in Oz can free me now. That's it.'

Frustrated, I looked down at the pavement. I no longer knew who was right: Collins or me. Looking up again, I said, 'If you try fighting them now, Jack, they'll kill you.'

'But they won't beat me.'

'You'll die.'

'On my feet. Not on my knees.'

'Jack – '

'Go back, White, across that street. Then stay behind that car. You're not, after all, such a bad one, so I'd rather you didn't get hurt. You hear me, White? Get moving… And stay clear.'

'Is your life that little?'

'What life? I never had a life. That's the one thing they managed to keep from me. White, if only…' His voice seemed to break, I heard him cough, then he said, very soft now, 'Get going. Now. Stay clear. Wash yourself.'

The last sentence whipped me. Slowly, not too sure of my direction, I turned away and started back. Somewhere in the distance was the sound of traffic, but the screaming silence in this street deadened all. Ahead of me was the squad car with the red-and-blue light winking, on and off, on and off. The megaphone lay on the bonnet, just behind the inspector's hand, which now had a pistol in it. Around the inspector were a few more policemen, one with the tear-gas grenades in his hands, the others, the marksmen, with rifles. It was a scene from a movie I'd seen sometime. I pushed through the coppers and stood by the inspector's squad car. The inspector was now standing beside me.

'Well, Mr White?'

'He won't come out.'

'No, I didn't think he would. You don't kill a policeman and live.'

'You want to kill him?'

'I won't enjoy it, if that's what you mean.'

'But you want it.'

'Yes, if we don't do it, the court will. There's no way on earth he could get out of the charge. You think that's nasty? You tell me: What other protection has a copper got in this job?'

'Nice.'

'Sure.' He turned to the men who stood slightly in front of him and said, 'I'm going to give him one more blast with the megaphone. If he doesn't play ball, toss in a few tear-gas grenades. You two take a bead on the door for when he comes out, if he does. If he looks like he's shooting, cut him down.'

'Looks like he's coming out,' a marksman said.

All heads turned to see the front door opening slowly, tentatively. There was a bare bulb shining somewhere back in that hallway, throwing a weak, yellow glow over a silhouetted figure that gradually became framed in the doorway. Then Collins was standing there, his hands above his head, the pistol clearly visible.

'Surprise, surprise,' the inspector said, setting down his pistol and lifting up the megaphone. Then his voice blared across the street: 'The pistol, fella! Let it go!'

Collins stepped forward into the large, bright beam of a spotlight that was fixed to the roof of one of the squad cars. His hands were still above his head, the right one still holding the pistol. He stopped again. Slowly, he turned his head to look in both directions at the solid ring of policemen. There was no way to break out and he knew it. Still, he didn't move; and the pistol remained pointing into the air above his head. Beside me, two marksmen went down to the kneeling position, the firing position, and took aim. I heard the safety catches clicking off. Then silence.

'Well, well,' Collins said, with a loud, clear, ringing voice, 'this sure is some show of strength.'

Then he lowered his pistol and fired.

It was almost as if he had been punched in the gut by an invisible fist. His stomach went inward, he was slammed back against the door-frame, his arms went jerking across each other with the pistol flying to the pavement, and it was only then I realised that the two marksmen had opened fire, the sound of the shots ringing in my eardrums. I blinked my eyes a few times, focused, then saw Collins fall forward onto his knees, one hand outstretched and desperately groping for the iron railing at the side of the steps. The marksmen had only fired once; they did not fire again. Collins' desperate fingers found the wet iron railing, took firm hold, started pulling. His knees came slightly off the top step, he swayed from side to side, his head flopped backward, and then his grip on the railing was lost, his hand trailing away. He shuddered and fell forward, face down, head splitting on the concrete edge of the bottom step. He didn't move again.

'He deliberately shot high,' the inspector said, then, slowly, all the policemen moved in on the body.

When I looked around, I saw Laura in the distance, standing by the squad car at the top of the street. I started walking in that direction, but the ground seemed to give way beneath me. I felt myself go down onto my knees. It came to me that I hadn't slept for three days and I smiled at that, and then I passed out.

When I came to, I was in the police station and I was crying – crying for Collins.

Chapter Eight

CIRCUIT COMPLETE

The next few days were pretty rough. With Laura I was in and out of the local police station like a boomerang, answering questions, giving statements, and signing papers that seemingly had no relevance to the case in hand. I became uneasily familiar with legal routine and certainly nervous in the growing awareness of what could be done to a man who was trapped in this administrative jungle.

Laura was quiet and remote through it all, speaking only when spoken to, responding to questions in a flat, dull monotone. When I spoke to her, she would smile encouragingly, but then retreat back into some ultimately unreadable private world. Whether she loved me or hated me, I couldn't quite tell. When asked about this, she was studiously non-committal.

It was only two weeks, but it seemed like years, when the police inspector finally said, 'Congratulations. You're now free to go.' I took Laura for a cup of coffee and she stared into the middle-distance. I tried not to think of the deaths of her brother and Jack Collins when I put the all-important question to her.

'Why?' she replied.

'Why *what*?'

'Why should I marry you?'

'Because I *want* you to. Because I want you living with me. I want you around all the time.'

'Why? Because you're frightened of being lonely again?'

'Yes. Aren't you?'

'Yes. That's *why* I wont marry you.'

'That doesn't make sense.'

'Disappear for a month. Think about it. If it starts to make sense, come back and try your luck again.'

'Try my luck?'

'I can't guarantee anything. You see, I *want* to marry you, but right now I'm not sure of my reasons. So I need the month, too.'

'You're crazy.'

'A month. Think about it. Now disappear.'

I was furious. Disappointed. I felt as bitter as hell. We unravel one mystery only to find another. I would have slapped her face there and then, but I knew for a fact that she wasn't just playing the old hard-to-get game. I tried to work out what she meant by this, but I wasn't up to thinking about it; I didn't really want to face what she *might* have meant.

So I started running again.

For two or three days, I floated around Sydney on a sea of booze, then I staggered onto a train heading for Queensland and stepped out of the platform of Brisbane station with watery, bloodshot eyes. It was as hot as hell up there and I nearly puked every time I stepped into the sunlight, so I took the next train going back. By this time I was in no mood for amiable conversation, I really felt like a good fight, and so I had a few problems with the conductor when he came through the carriage to check the tickets. I got off the train at Sydney and stayed just long enough to catch the next train to Melbourne. Eventually disembarking there, I resolved to find myself a loose woman with low morals, but I was too drunk to have much appeal. Instead, I just walked the streets again, falling in and out of bars, and thinking of Laura's parting words.

'*A month. Think about it. Now disappear.*'

It was a mystery, no two ways about it, and it had vague hints of something that had been said between us in earlier, now more distant, times, but I'd be damned if I could think of what it was. All I knew was that I wanted her. When I tried to imagine a future without her, I instantly felt suicidal. Certainly, as she had suggested, I didn't want to be alone anymore. I was fearful of nights spent in isolation. I was afraid of what might happen to me if she wasn't there to lean... yes, lean on, lean on.

I caught a train out of Melbourne and watched the city falling away behind me in the lonesome night, and then there was nothing but the Nullarbor Plain again, that great desert expanse brooding silently under a star-bright sky. *Don't run*! cried the voice in my head, but I wanted to dive through the carriage window and run screaming across that vast, dark wilderness where no one would ever find me again and I could die in peace, thinking of nothing... nothing except her upon whom I could lean... yes, lean on... out of my pitiful need, my weak, cowardly, parasitical need.

Yes, I finally knew what she had meant.

The train kept rolling on across the desert, steel tracks etching a grey parallel into the coming day, and I leaned back in my seat, knocked off the drinking, and tried to face the rising sun. This wasn't easy, but eventually I managed it, and then I started to think about the whole damned mess, and to face up to it, as well as to the rising sun, and to work out exactly what was wrong. Then the sun rose high in the sky, the air had a shimmering radiance, I successfully swallowed a sandwich, and I knew, sure as the fact that I was going to go back, that I wasn't frightened anymore; that what I had been through was a catharsis, that finally I was cleansed and could brave the wind, no matter how fierce it might be, no matter how cruelly it might blow.

And then I also knew that although I wanted Laura, and wanted her badly, I no longer needed her to help me face my unresolved future.

When I got off the train at Perth, I was almost on my knees, not with alcoholism, but with pure physical exhaustion. Again, I hadn't slept for days.

I went home, rang the doorbell, and initially faced the icy reproof of my mother and sister. It wasn't easy, but I spent almost a month there, talking, smiling, wriggling out of the Purgatory I had created for myself, letting them see that I was not the man I had been; until finally they came around, their former warmth returning, and then I told them I was going back to Sydney and also told them why. They wished me good luck.

The journey back seemed to take years, but it didn't bother me much. I knew exactly where I was going and why, and this time I was running *to*, not *from*. It was a new experience for me, so when I disembarked at Sydney, I grabbed my travel bag, not forgetting my typewriter, caught a cab, gave the driver the address and tipped him rashly when we arrived there. I got out of the cab, sat my gear on the pavement opposite to where she lived, and then, folding my arms, clean-shaven and sober, I patiently waited.

After nearly six hours, she came walking along the street to the apartment block where she lived. Her raven hair was piled up on her head, as it had been when we first met, and she was wearing a white gaberdine. When I spoke to her, she turned around and she looked lovely. She didn't smile.

'I don't need you,' she said.

'I don't need *you*,' I said.

'I want you,' she said.

'I want you.'

She looked thoughtfully at me for what seemed like an eternity, and then, slowly, almost rapturously, her smile came up like the desert sun. Reaching down, I brought her right hand up to my lips. Then, in a mock salute to that which was past but could never be forgotten, I raised my hand to her bowing forehead.

'Welcome home,' she said.

Other books by W. A. Harbinson can be found at

www.waharbinson.eu.com

Made in United States
Orlando, FL
30 November 2025

73428223R20079